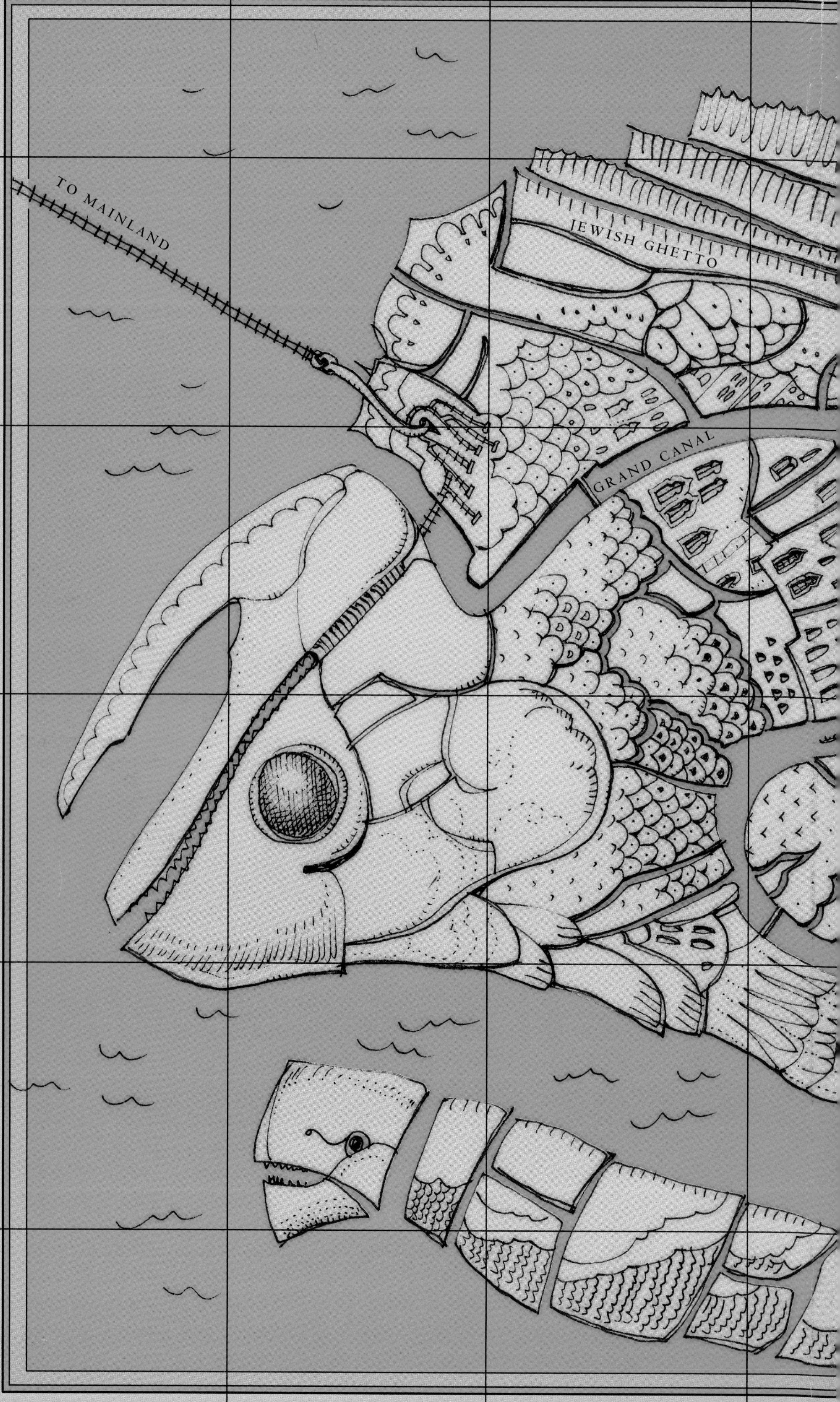
TO MAINLAND
JEWISH GHETTO
GRAND CANAL

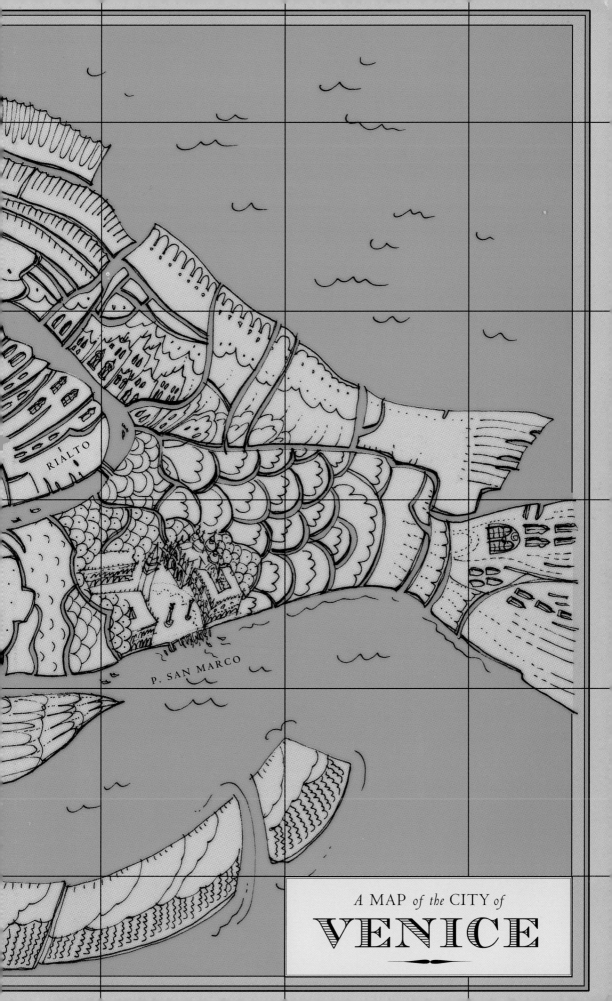

RIALTO

P. SAN MARCO

A MAP of the CITY of

VENICE

The
MERCHANT
of
VENICE

a play by William Shakespeare

adapted and illustrated by Gareth Hinds

CANDLEWICK PRESS
CAMBRIDGE, MASSACHUSETTS

DRAMATIS PERSONAE

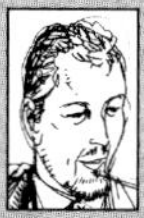

ANTONIO .... *a merchant of Venice*

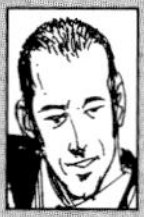

BASSANIO .... *his friend, suitor to Portia*

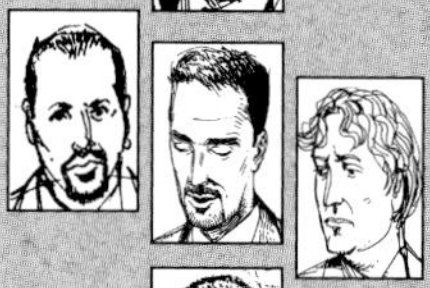

GRATIANO, SALERIO, SALANIO .... *friends to Antonio and Bassanio*

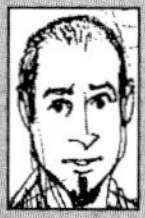

LORENZO .... *in love with Jessica*

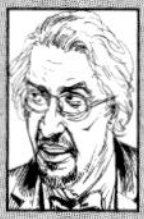

SHYLOCK .... *a rich Jew*

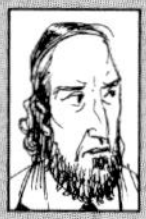

TUBAL .... *a Jew, his friend*

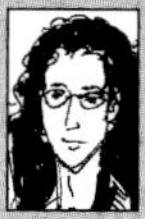

JESSICA .... *daughter to Shylock*

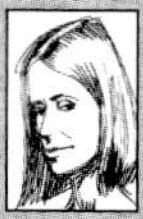

PORTIA .... *a rich heiress*

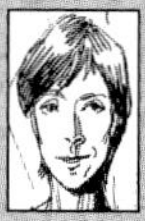

NERISSA .... *her waiting-maid*

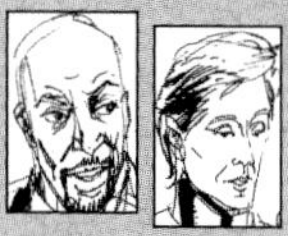

The Prince of MOROCCO, ... *suitors to Portia*
The Prince of ARAGON

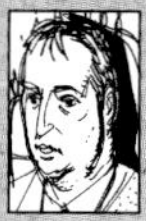

The Duke of VENICE

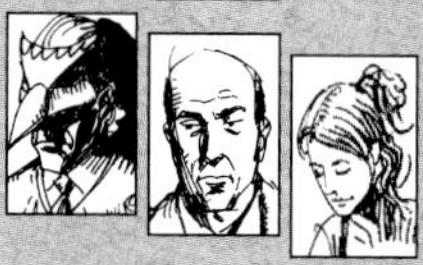

Magnificoes of Venice; officers of the Court of Justice; servants to Portia; and other attendants

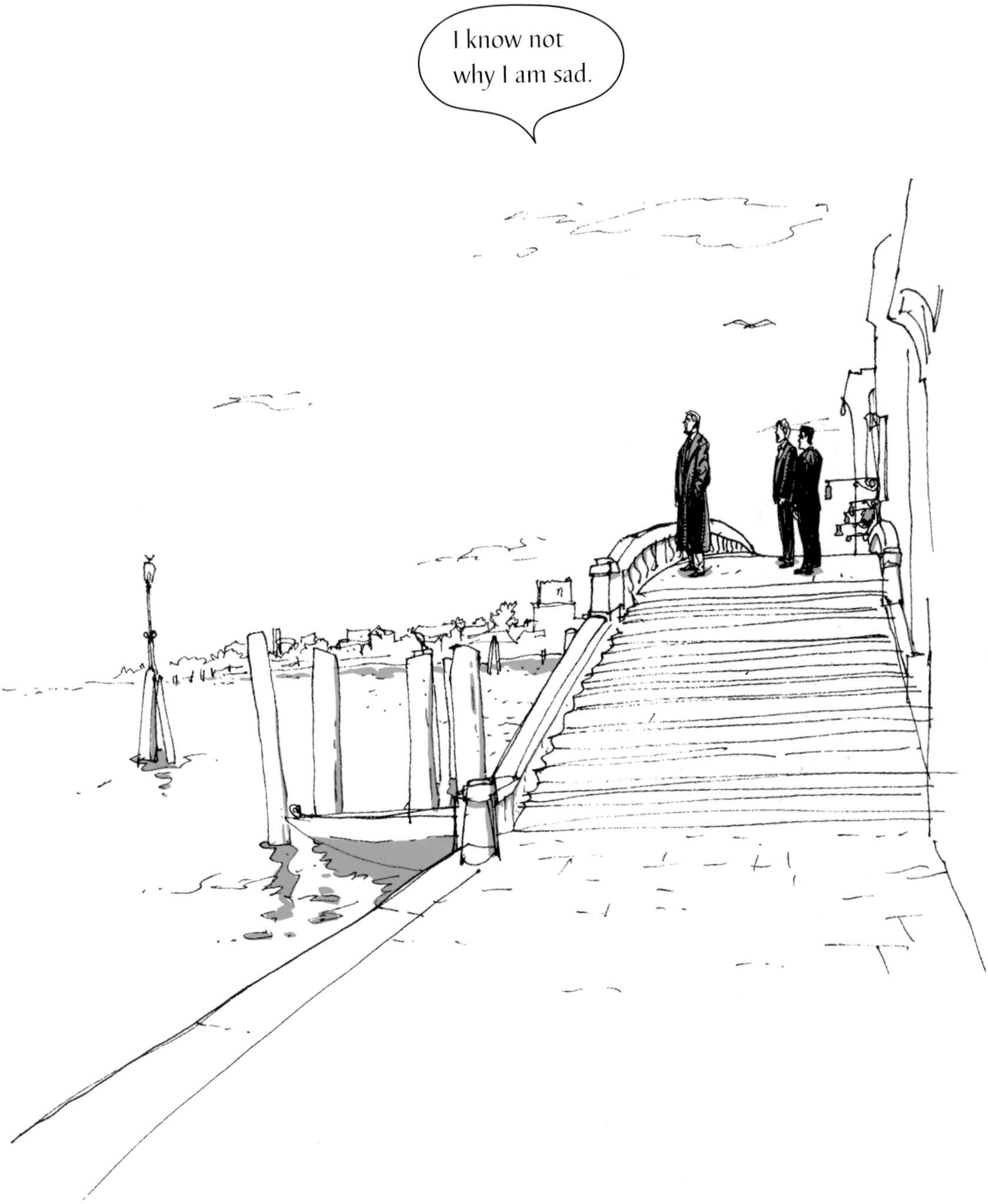
I know not
why I am sad.

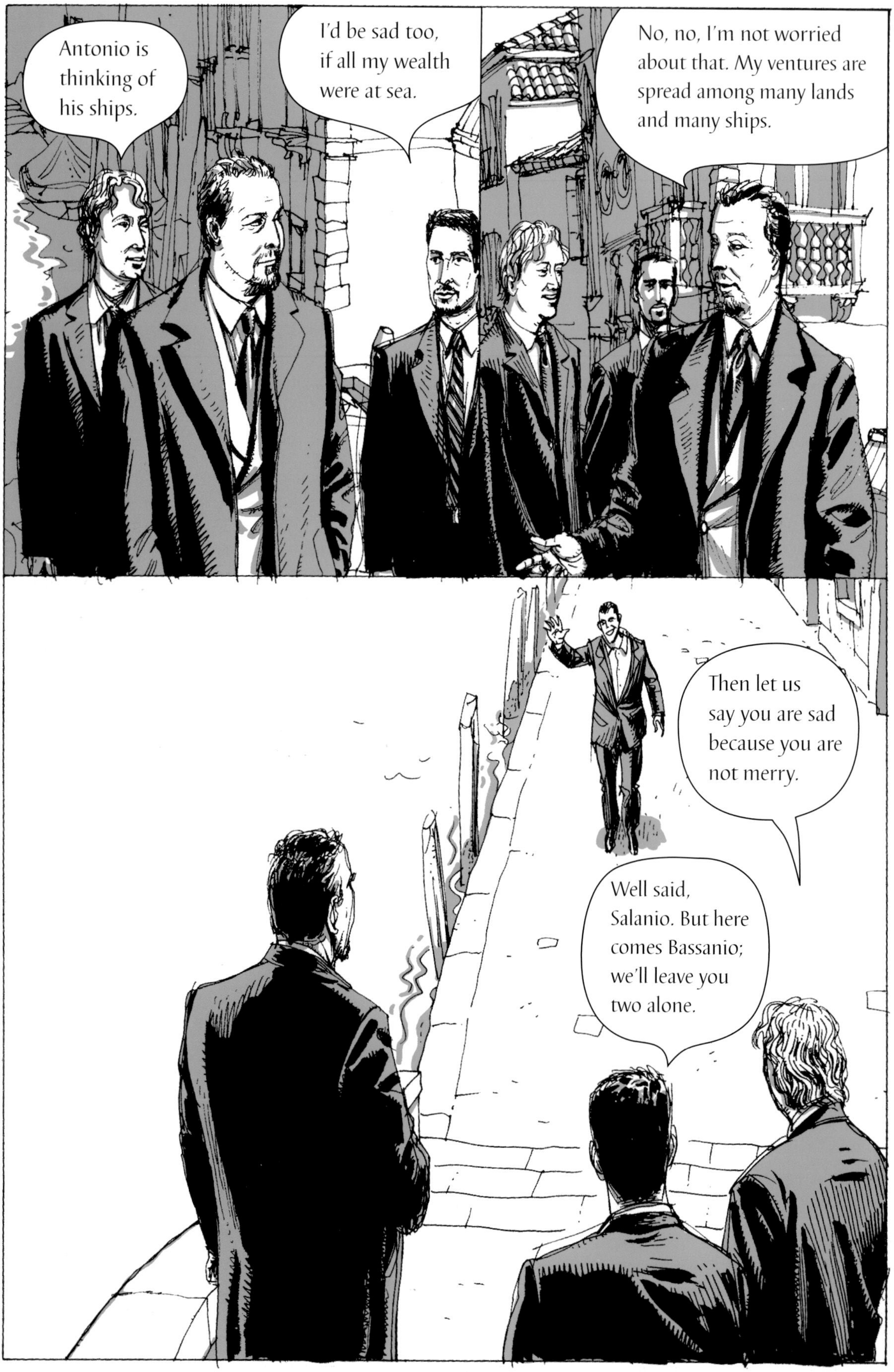
Antonio is thinking of his ships.
I'd be sad too, if all my wealth were at sea.
No, no, I'm not worried about that. My ventures are spread among many lands and many ships.
Then let us say you are sad because you are not merry.
Well said, Salanio. But here comes Bassanio; we'll leave you two alone.

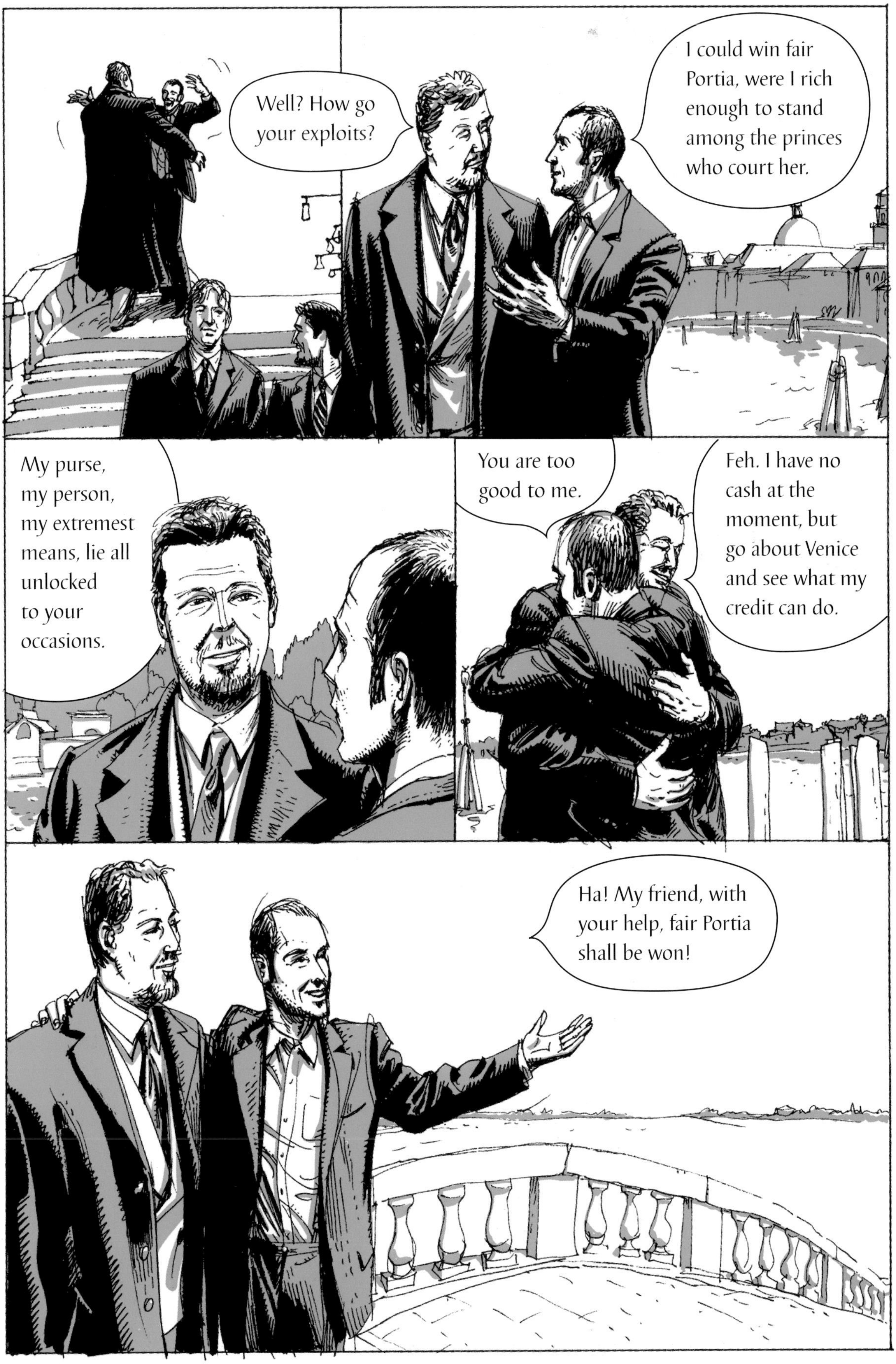
Well? How go your exploits?
I could win fair Portia, were I rich enough to stand among the princes who court her.
My purse, my person, my extremest means, lie all unlocked to your occasions.
You are too good to me.
Feh. I have no cash at the moment, but go about Venice and see what my credit can do.
Ha! My friend, with your help, fair Portia shall be won!

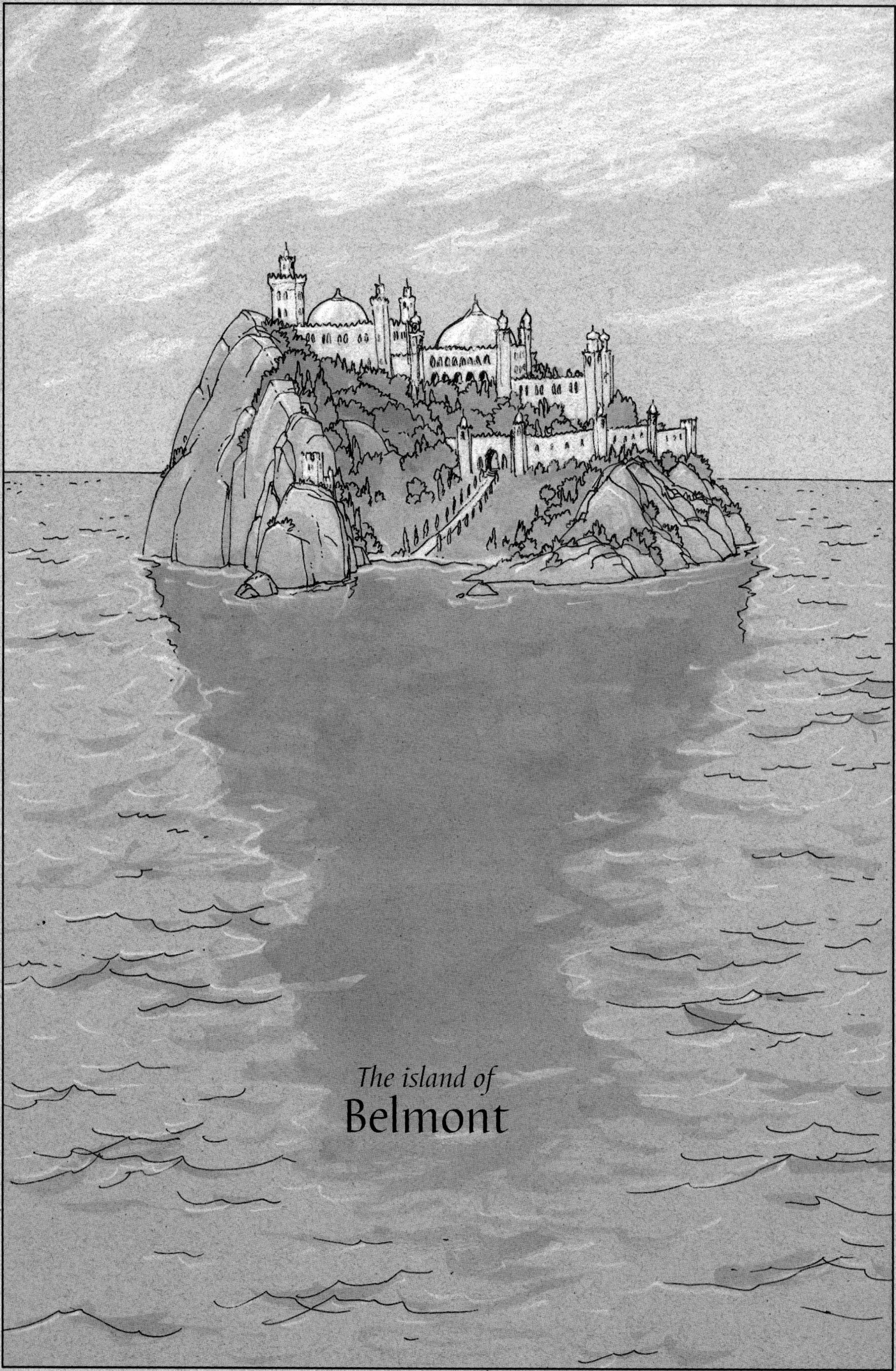
The island of
Belmont

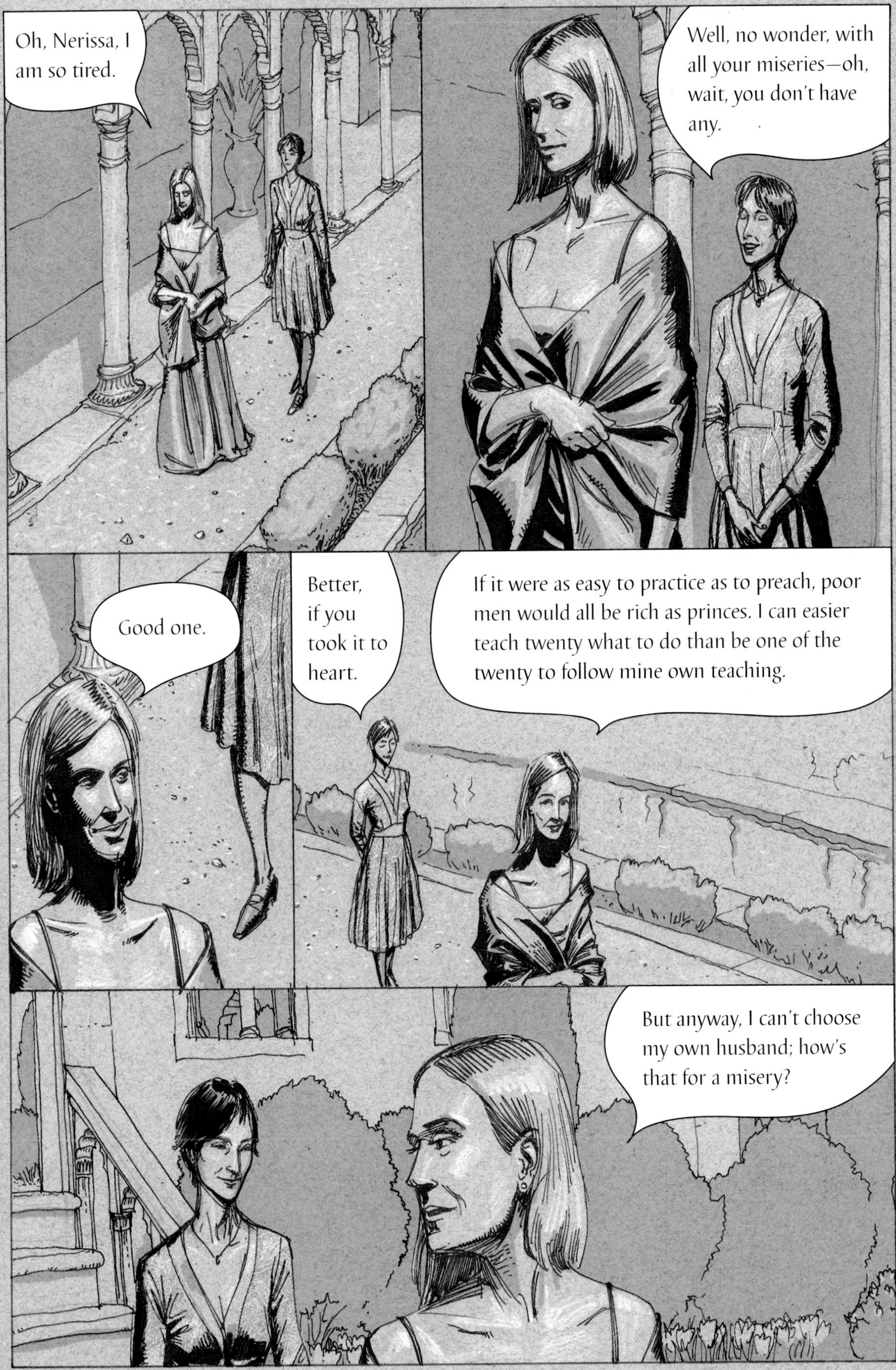
Oh, Nerissa, I am so tired.
Well, no wonder, with all your miseries—oh, wait, you don't have any.
Good one.
Better, if you took it to heart.
If it were as easy to practice as to preach, poor men would all be rich as princes. I can easier teach twenty what to do than be one of the twenty to follow mine own teaching.
But anyway, I can't choose my own husband; how's that for a misery?

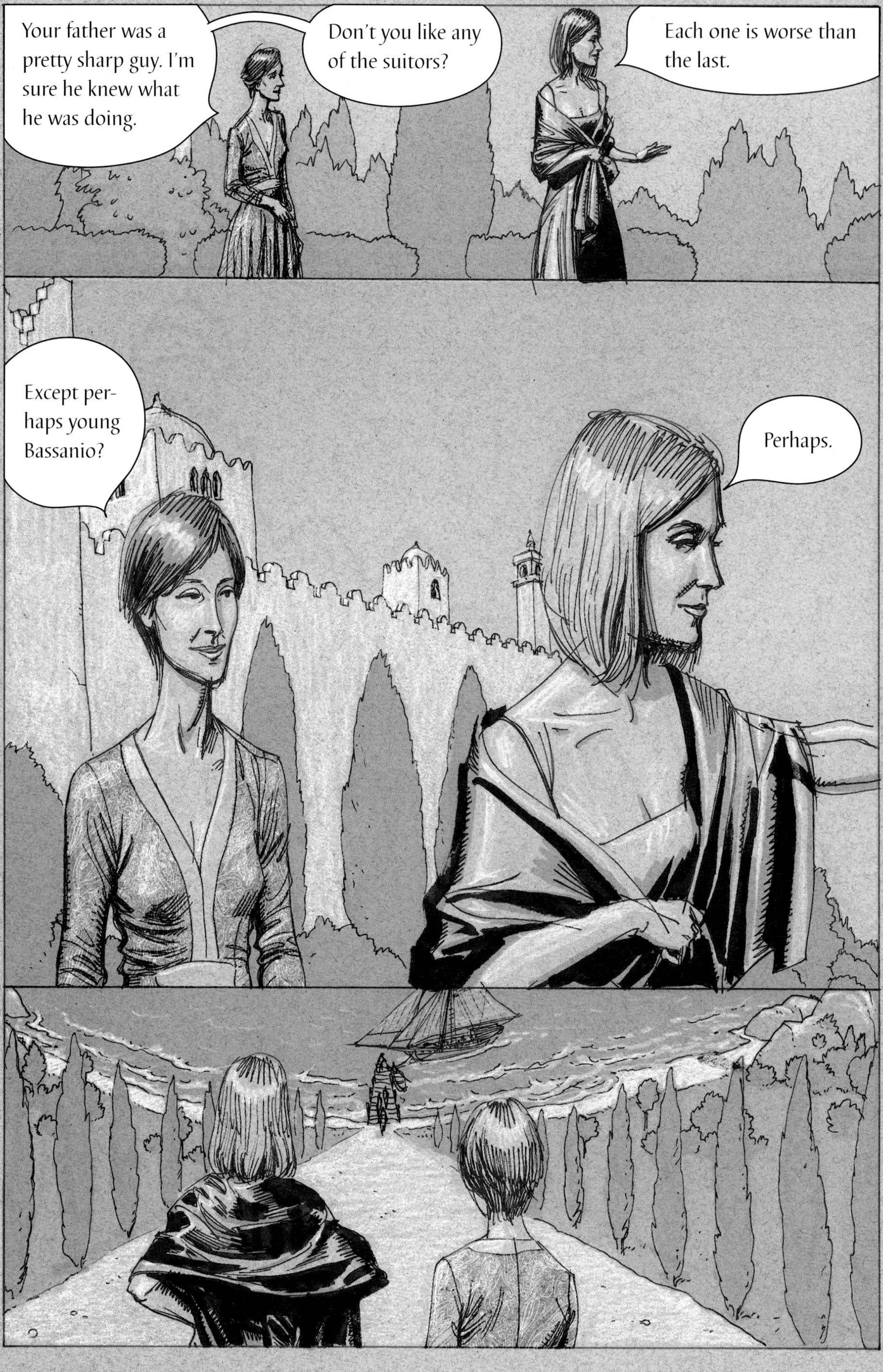
Your father was a pretty sharp guy. I'm sure he knew what he was doing.
Don't you like any of the suitors?
Each one is worse than the last.
Except per-haps young Bassanio?
Perhaps.

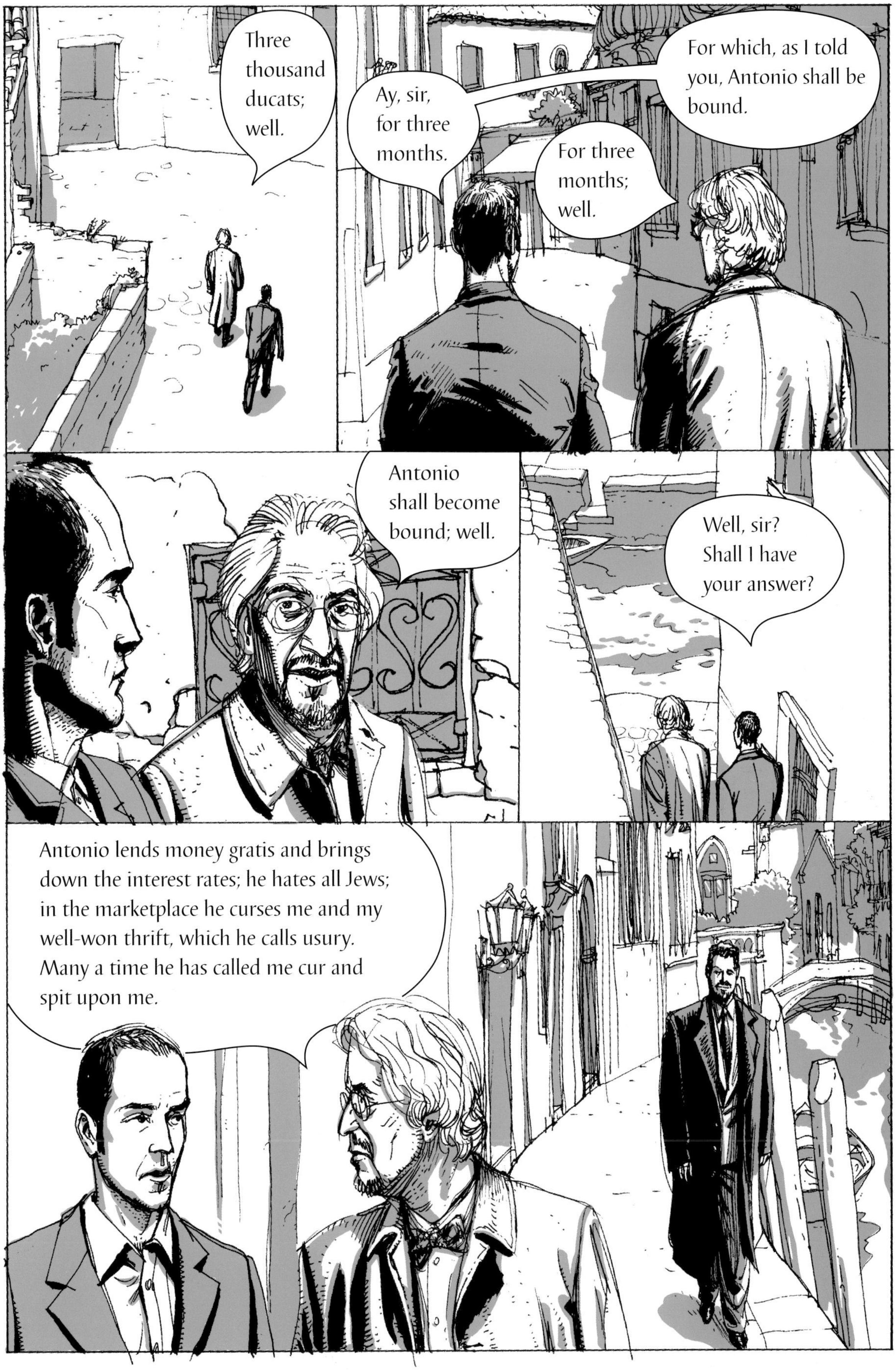
Three thousand ducats; well.
Ay, sir, for three months.
For three months; well.
For which, as I told you, Antonio shall be bound.
Antonio shall become bound; well.
Well, sir? Shall I have your answer?
Antonio lends money gratis and brings down the interest rates; he hates all Jews; in the marketplace he curses me and my well-won thrift, which he calls usury. Many a time he has called me cur and spit upon me.

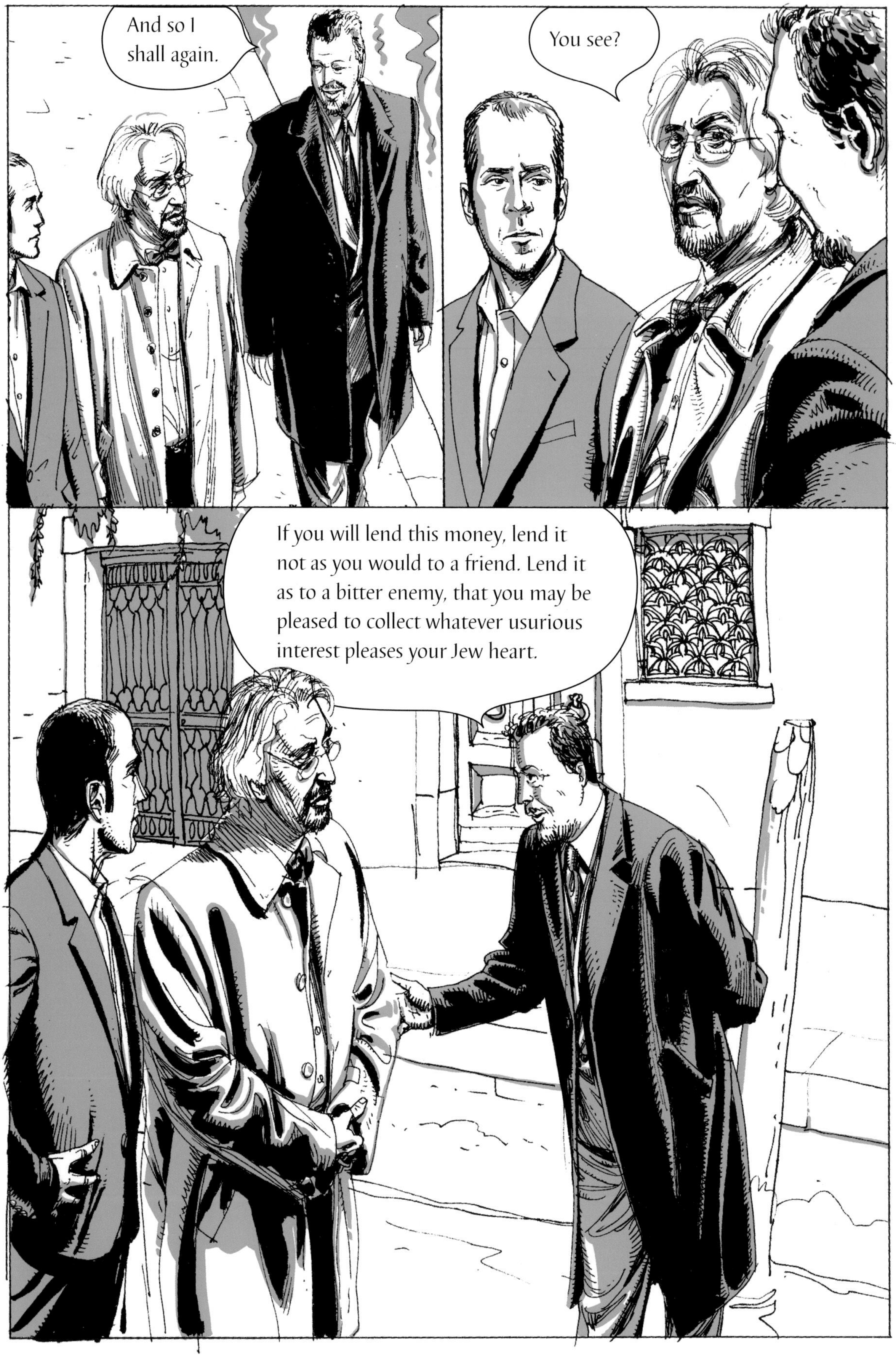
And so I shall again.
You see?
If you will lend this money, lend it not as you would to a friend. Lend it as to a bitter enemy, that you may be pleased to collect whatever usurious interest pleases your Jew heart.

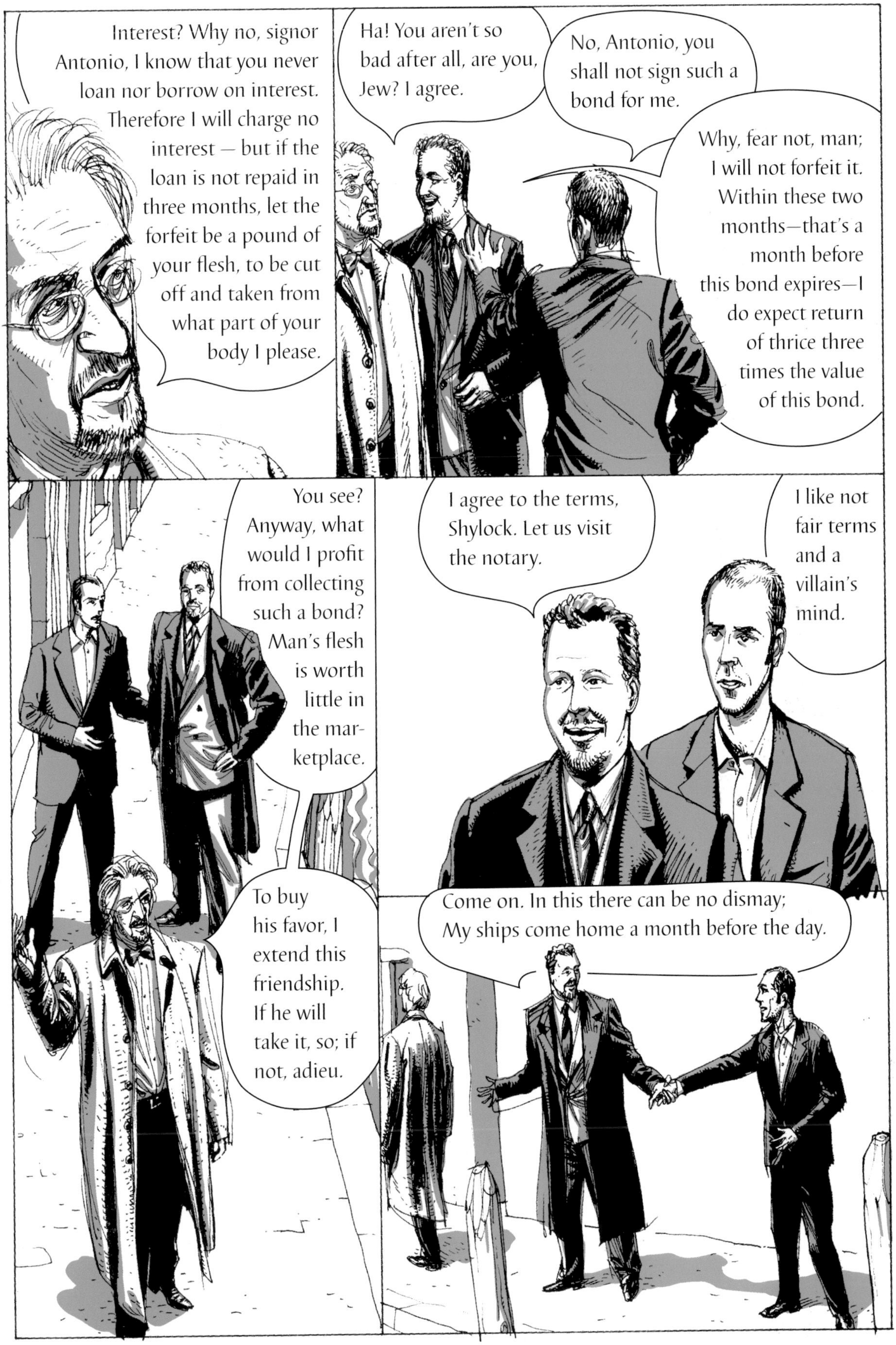
Interest? Why no, signor Antonio, I know that you never loan nor borrow on interest. Therefore I will charge no interest — but if the loan is not repaid in three months, let the forfeit be a pound of your flesh, to be cut off and taken from what part of your body I please.
Ha! You aren't so bad after all, are you, Jew? I agree.
No, Antonio, you shall not sign such a bond for me.
Why, fear not, man; I will not forfeit it. Within these two months—that's a month before this bond expires—I do expect return of thrice three times the value of this bond.
You see? Anyway, what would I profit from collecting such a bond? Man's flesh is worth little in the mar-ketplace.
To buy his favor, I extend this friendship. If he will take it, so; if not, adieu.
I agree to the terms, Shylock. Let us visit the notary.
I like not fair terms and a villain's mind.
Come on. In this there can be no dismay;
My ships come home a month before the day.

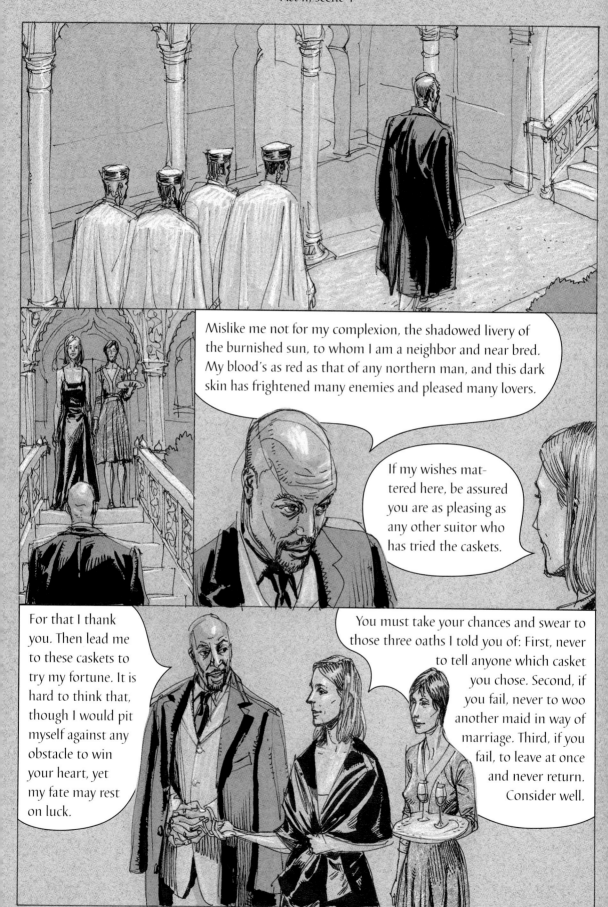

Mislike me not for my complexion, the shadowed livery of the burnished sun, to whom I am a neighbor and near bred. My blood's as red as that of any northern man, and this dark skin has frightened many enemies and pleased many lovers.

If my wishes mattered here, be assured you are as pleasing as any other suitor who has tried the caskets.

For that I thank you. Then lead me to these caskets to try my fortune. It is hard to think that, though I would pit myself against any obstacle to win your heart, yet my fate may rest on luck.

You must take your chances and swear to those three oaths I told you of: First, never to tell anyone which casket you chose. Second, if you fail, never to woo another maid in way of marriage. Third, if you fail, to leave at once and never return. Consider well.

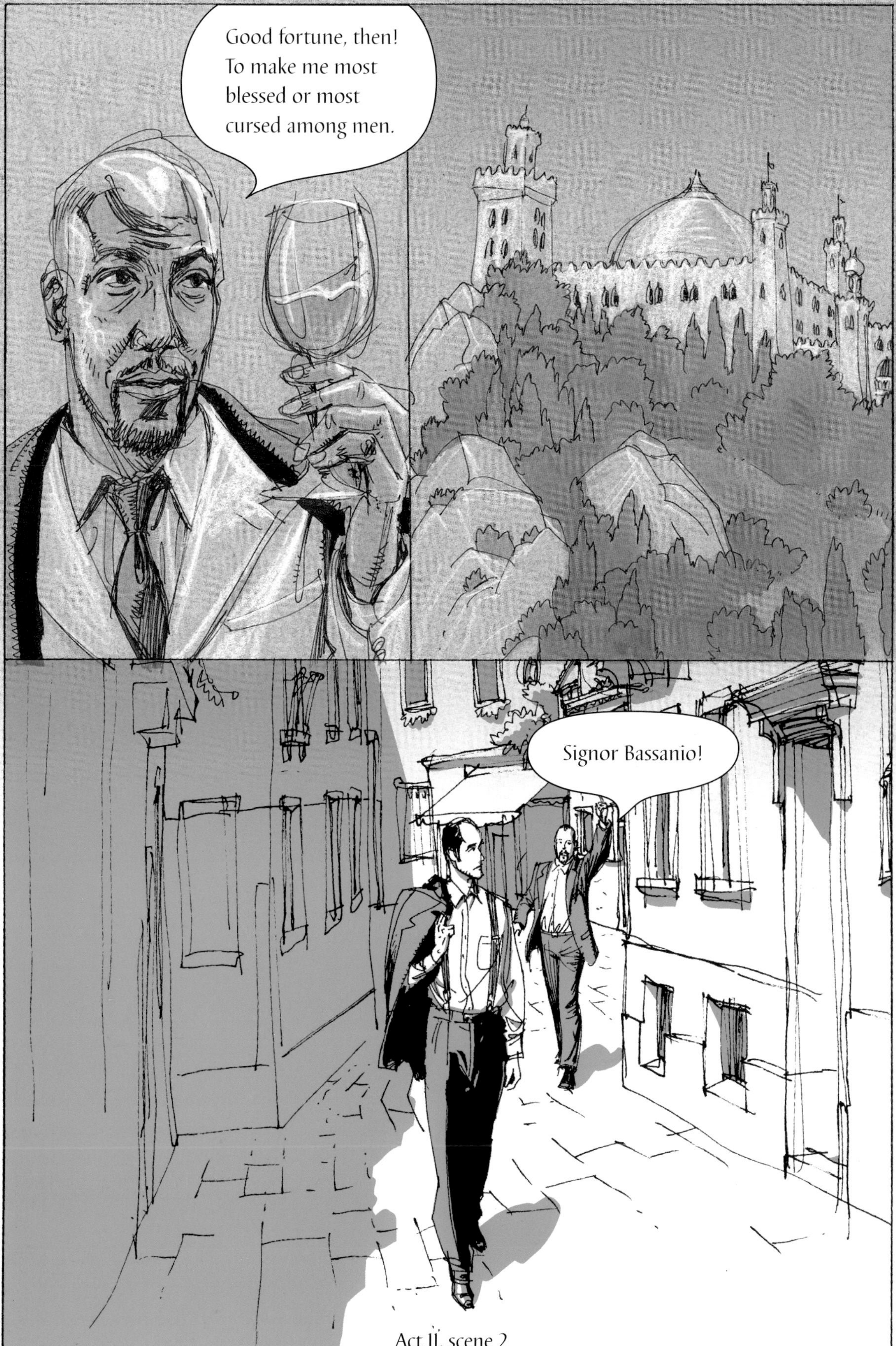
Good fortune, then! To make me most blessed or most cursed among men.
Signor Bassanio!
Act II, scene 2

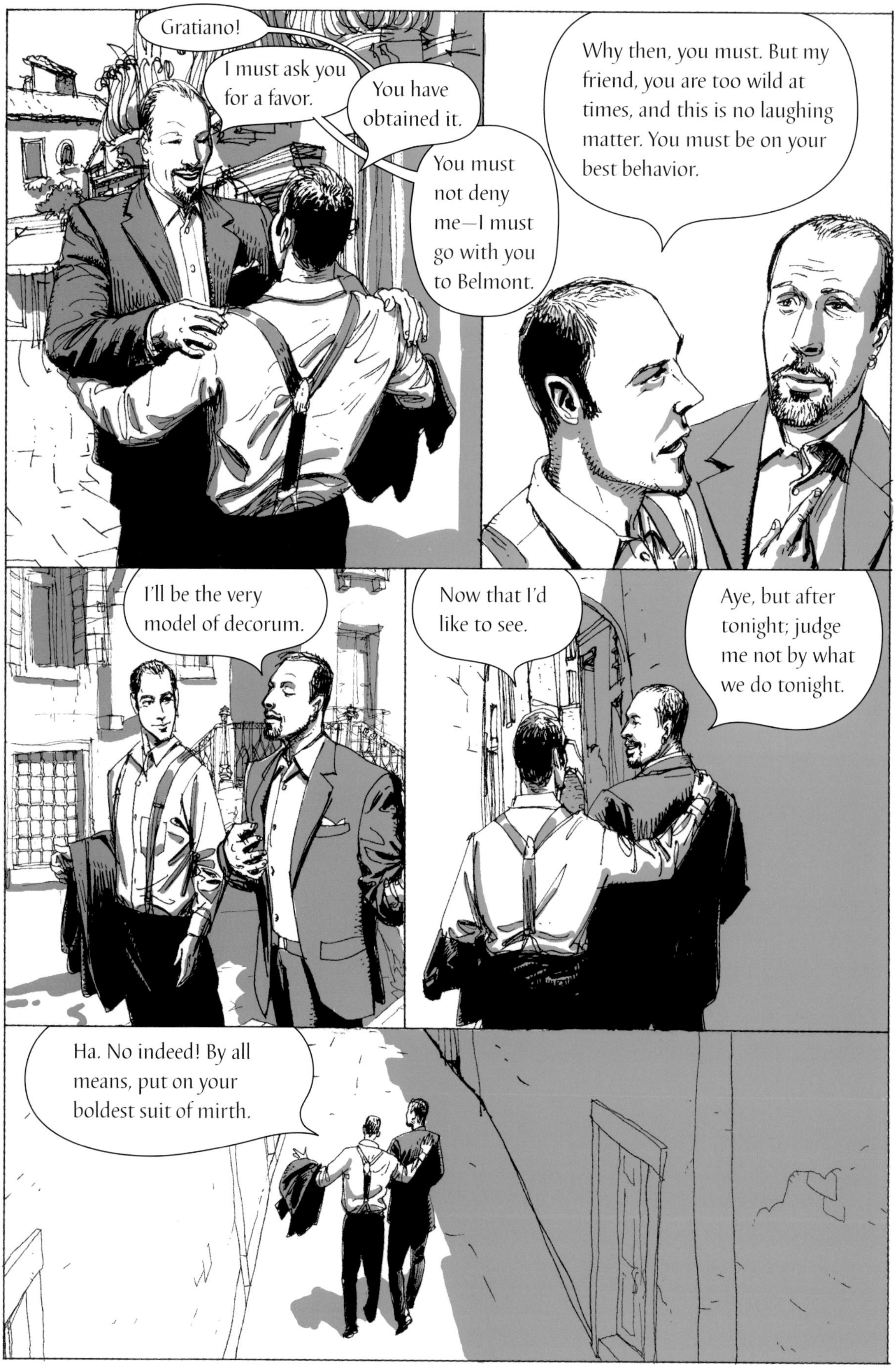
Gratiano!
I must ask you for a favor.
You have obtained it.
You must not deny me—I must go with you to Belmont.
Why then, you must. But my friend, you are too wild at times, and this is no laughing matter. You must be on your best behavior.
I'll be the very model of decorum.
Now that I'd like to see.
Aye, but after tonight; judge me not by what we do tonight.
Ha. No indeed! By all means, put on your boldest suit of mirth.

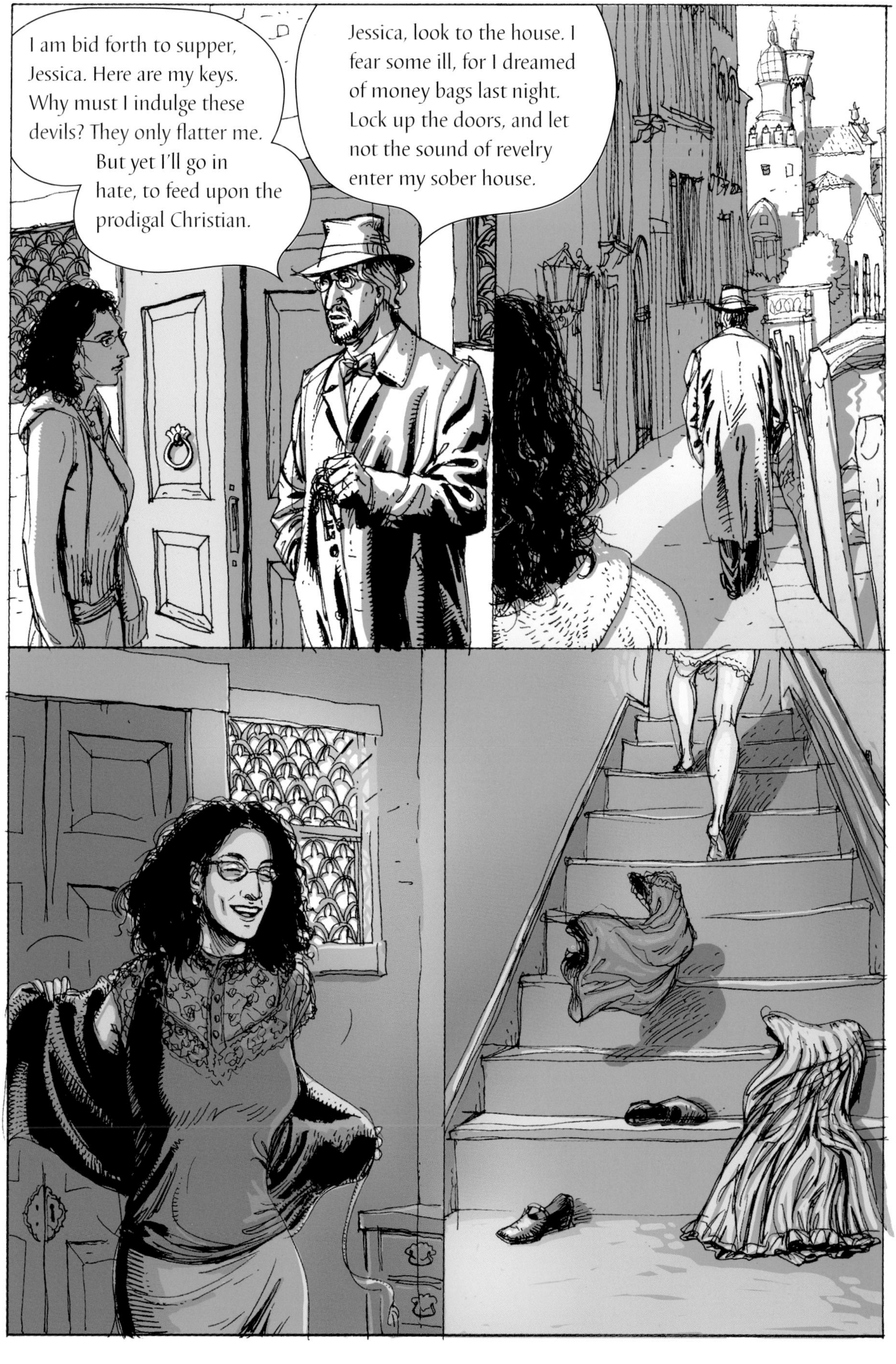
I am bid forth to supper, Jessica. Here are my keys. Why must I indulge these devils? They only flatter me. But yet I'll go in hate, to feed upon the prodigal Christian.
Jessica, look to the house. I fear some ill, for I dreamed of money bags last night. Lock up the doors, and let not the sound of revelry enter my sober house.

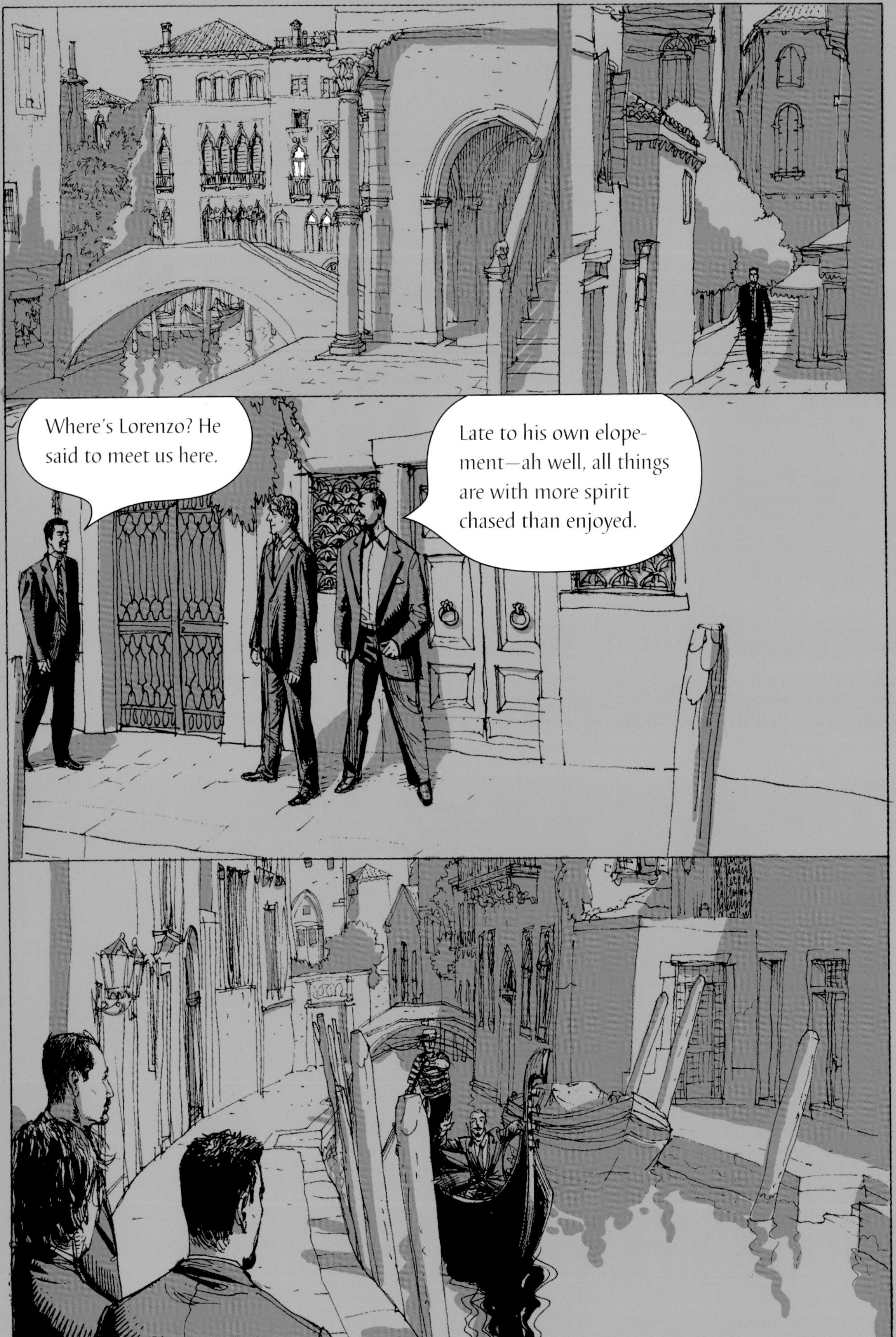
Where's Lorenzo? He said to meet us here.
Late to his own elopement—ah well, all things are with more spirit chased than enjoyed.

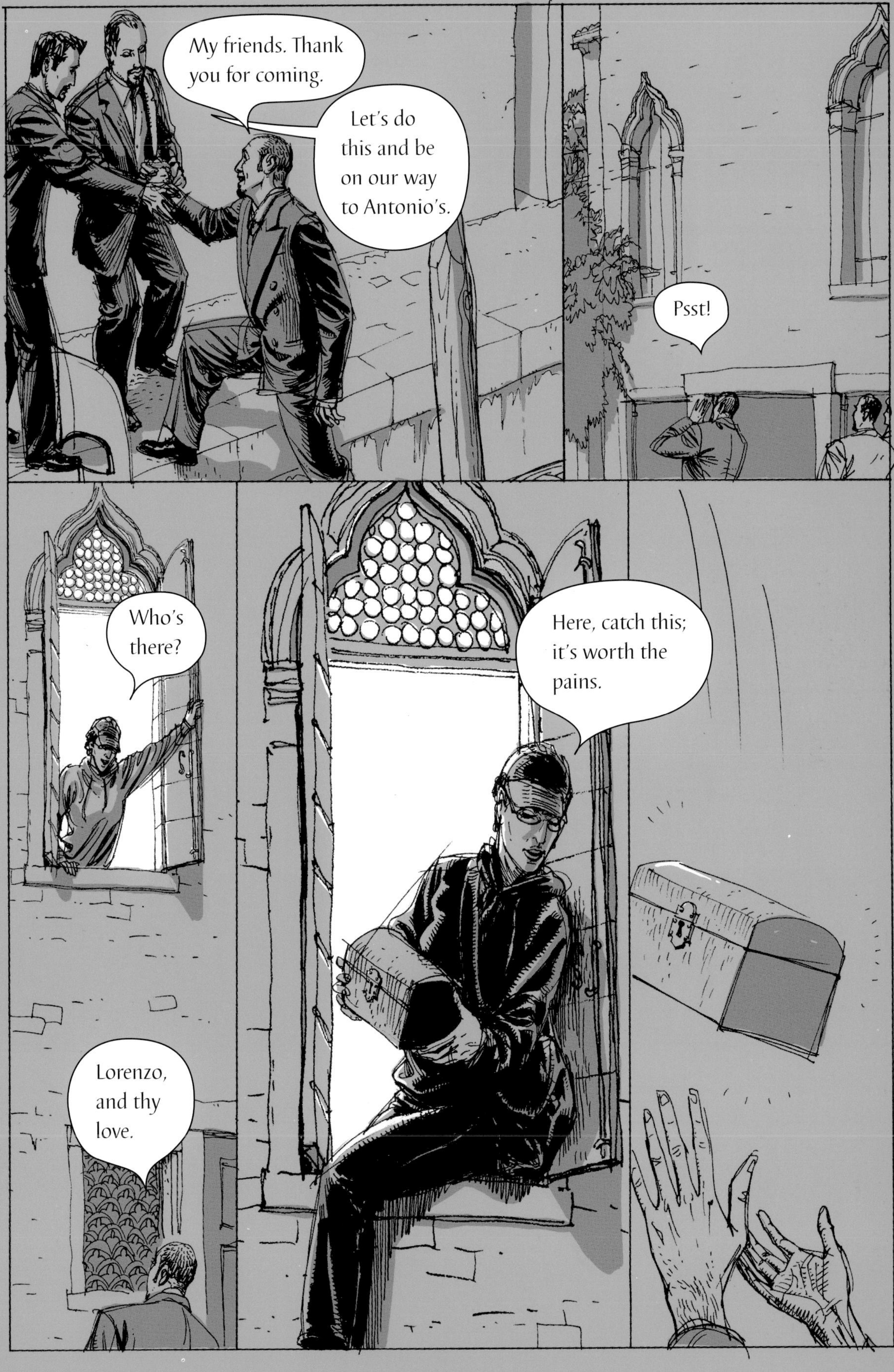
My friends. Thank you for coming.
Let's do this and be on our way to Antonio's.
Psst!
Who's there?
Lorenzo, and thy love.
Here, catch this; it's worth the pains.

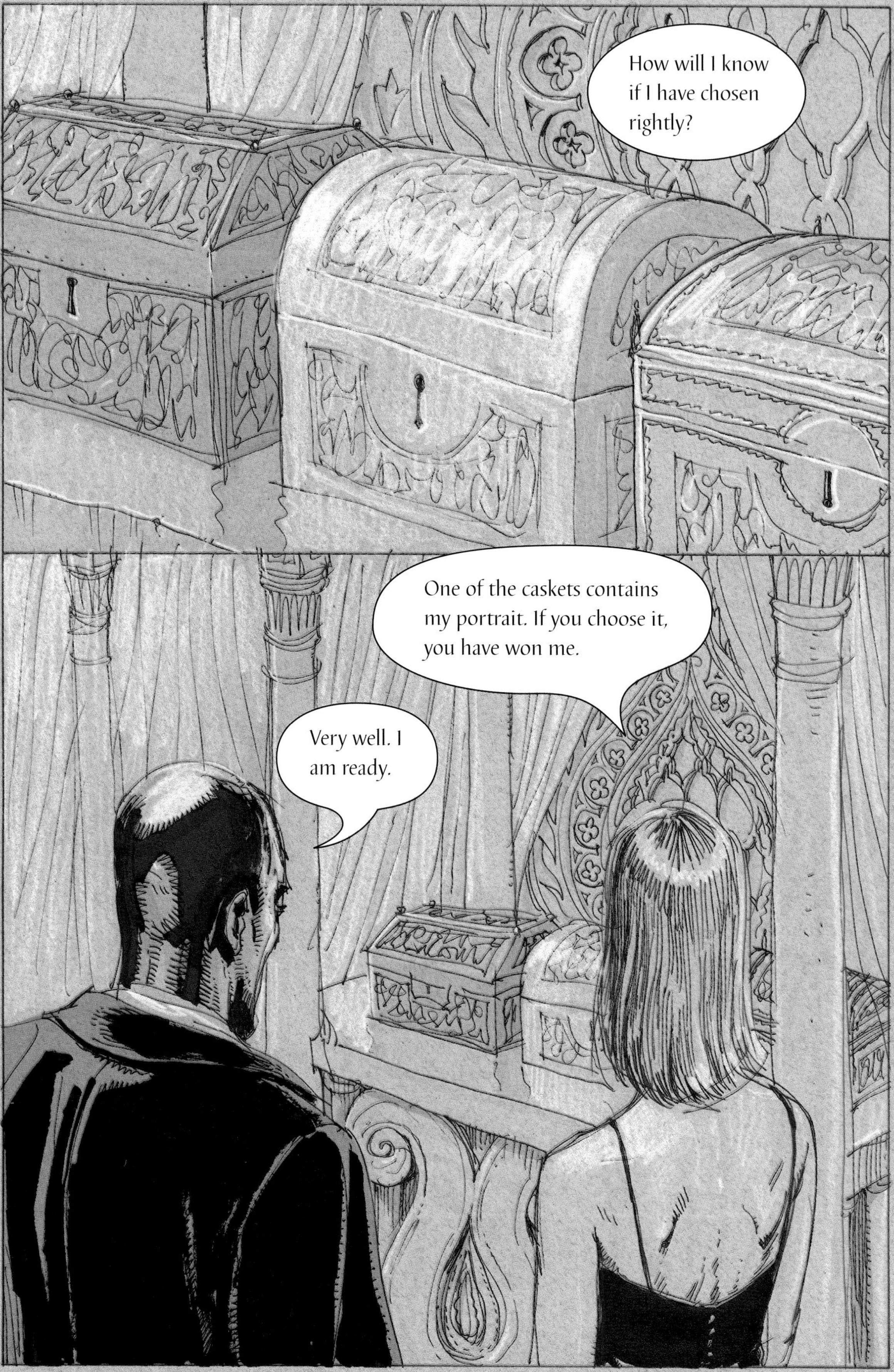
How will I know if I have chosen rightly?
One of the caskets contains my portrait. If you choose it, you have won me.
Very well. I am ready.

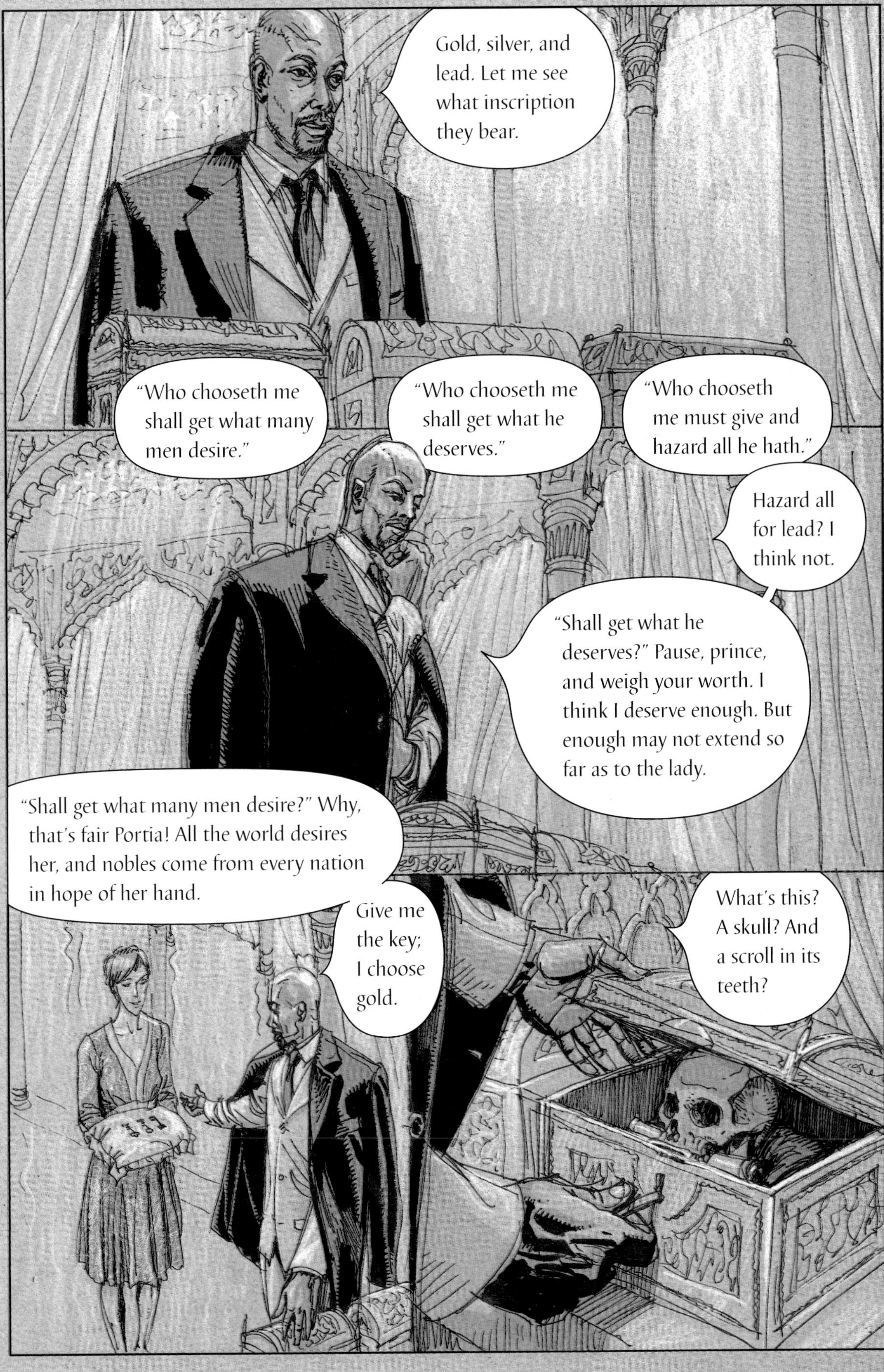
Gold, silver, and lead. Let me see what inscription they bear.
"Who chooseth me shall get what many men desire."
"Who chooseth me shall get what he deserves."
"Who chooseth me must give and hazard all he hath."
Hazard all for lead? I think not.
"Shall get what he deserves?" Pause, prince, and weigh your worth. I think I deserve enough. But enough may not extend so far as to the lady.
"Shall get what many men desire?" Why, that's fair Portia! All the world desires her, and nobles come from every nation in hope of her hand.
Give me the key; I choose gold.
What's this? A skull? And a scroll in its teeth?

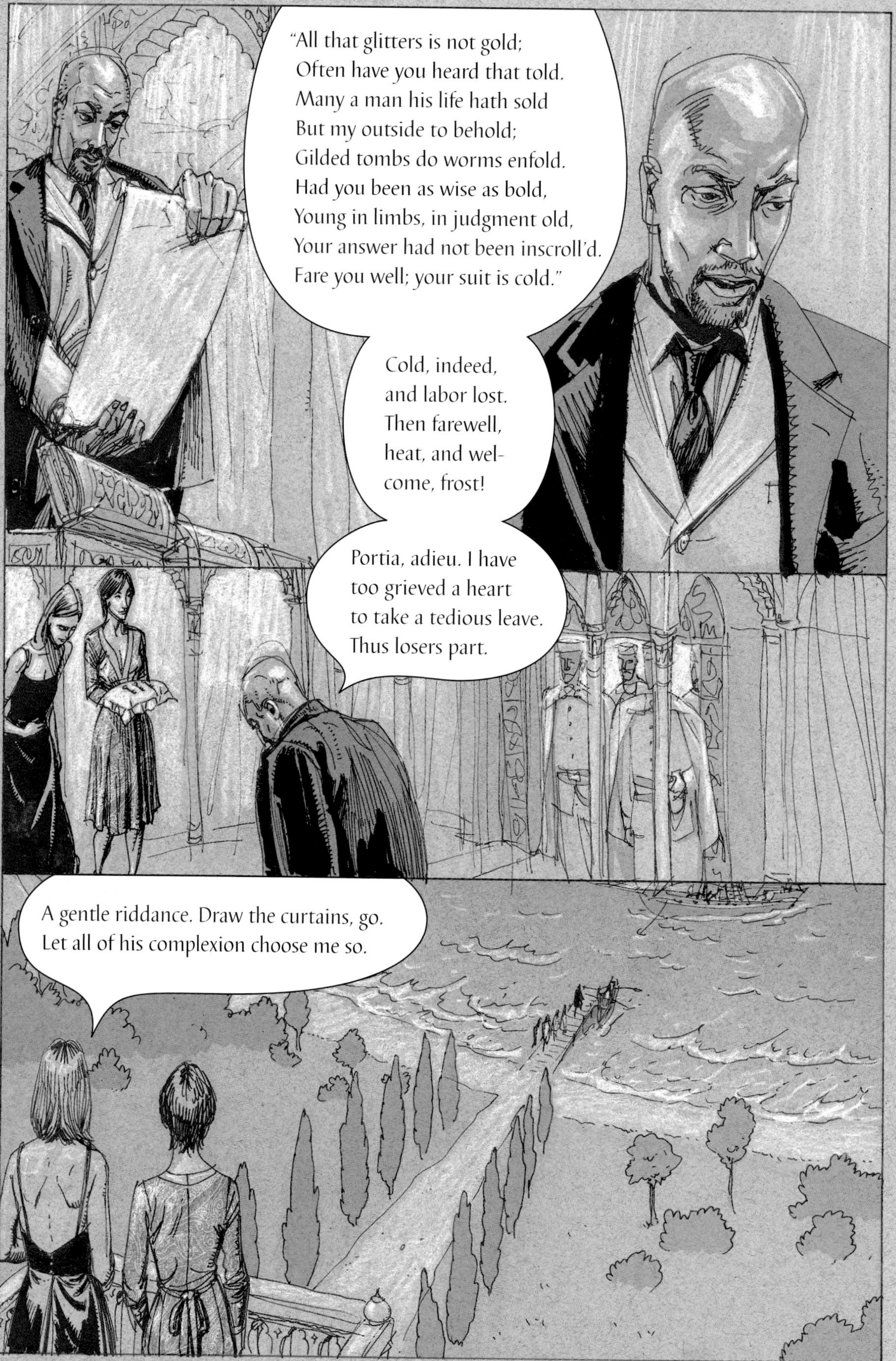
"All that glitters is not gold;
Often have you heard that told.
Many a man his life hath sold
But my outside to behold;
Gilded tombs do worms enfold.
Had you been as wise as bold,
Young in limbs, in judgment old,
Your answer had not been inscroll'd.
Fare you well; your suit is cold."
Cold, indeed, and labor lost. Then farewell, heat, and wel-come, frost!
Portia, adieu. I have too grieved a heart to take a tedious leave. Thus losers part.
A gentle riddance. Draw the curtains, go. Let all of his complexion choose me so.

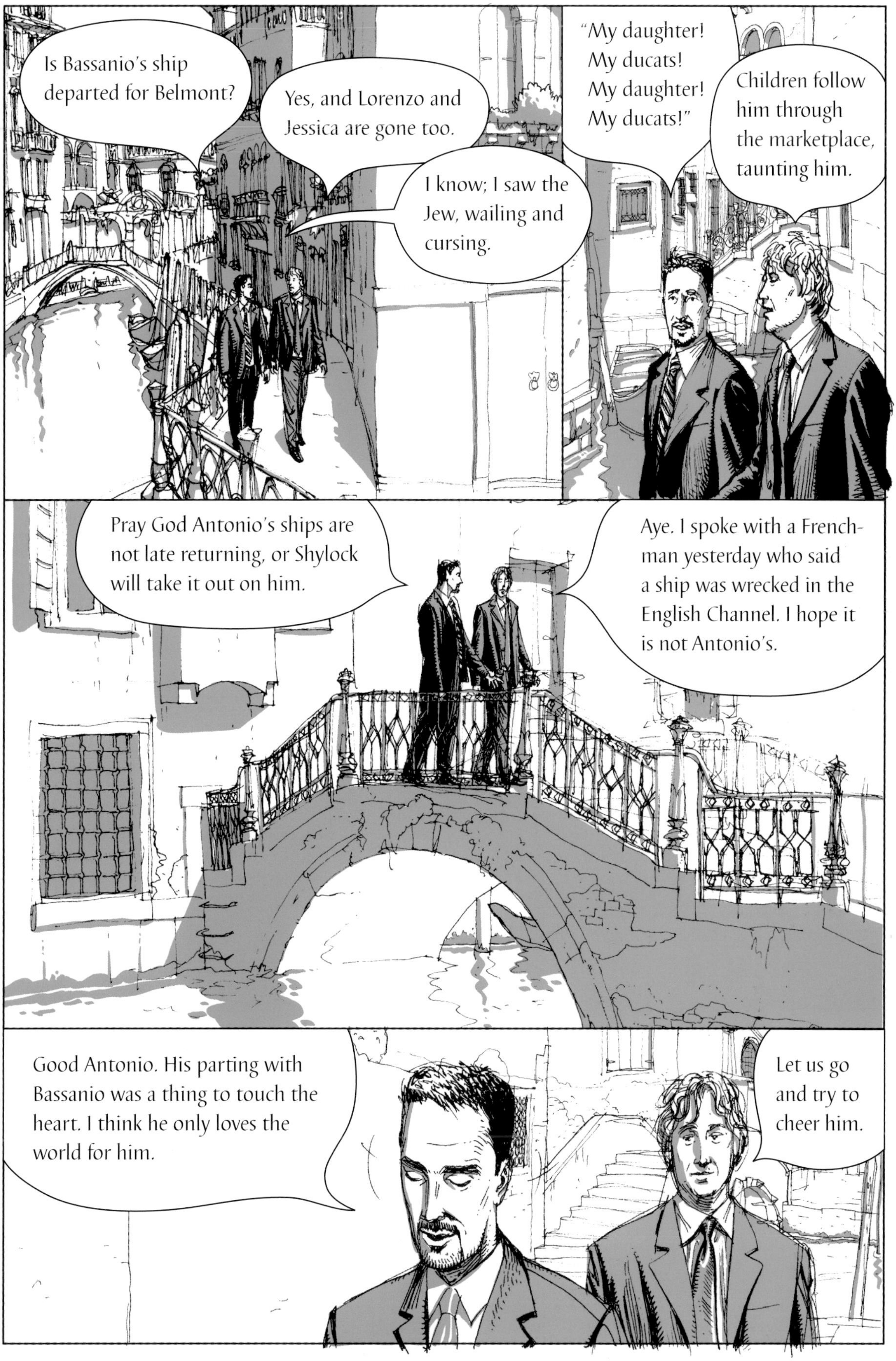
Is Bassanio's ship departed for Belmont?
Yes, and Lorenzo and Jessica are gone too.
I know; I saw the Jew, wailing and cursing.
"My daughter! My ducats! My daughter! My ducats!"
Children follow him through the marketplace, taunting him.
Pray God Antonio's ships are not late returning, or Shylock will take it out on him.
Aye. I spoke with a French-man yesterday who said a ship was wrecked in the English Channel. I hope it is not Antonio's.
Good Antonio. His parting with Bassanio was a thing to touch the heart. I think he only loves the world for him.
Let us go and try to cheer him.

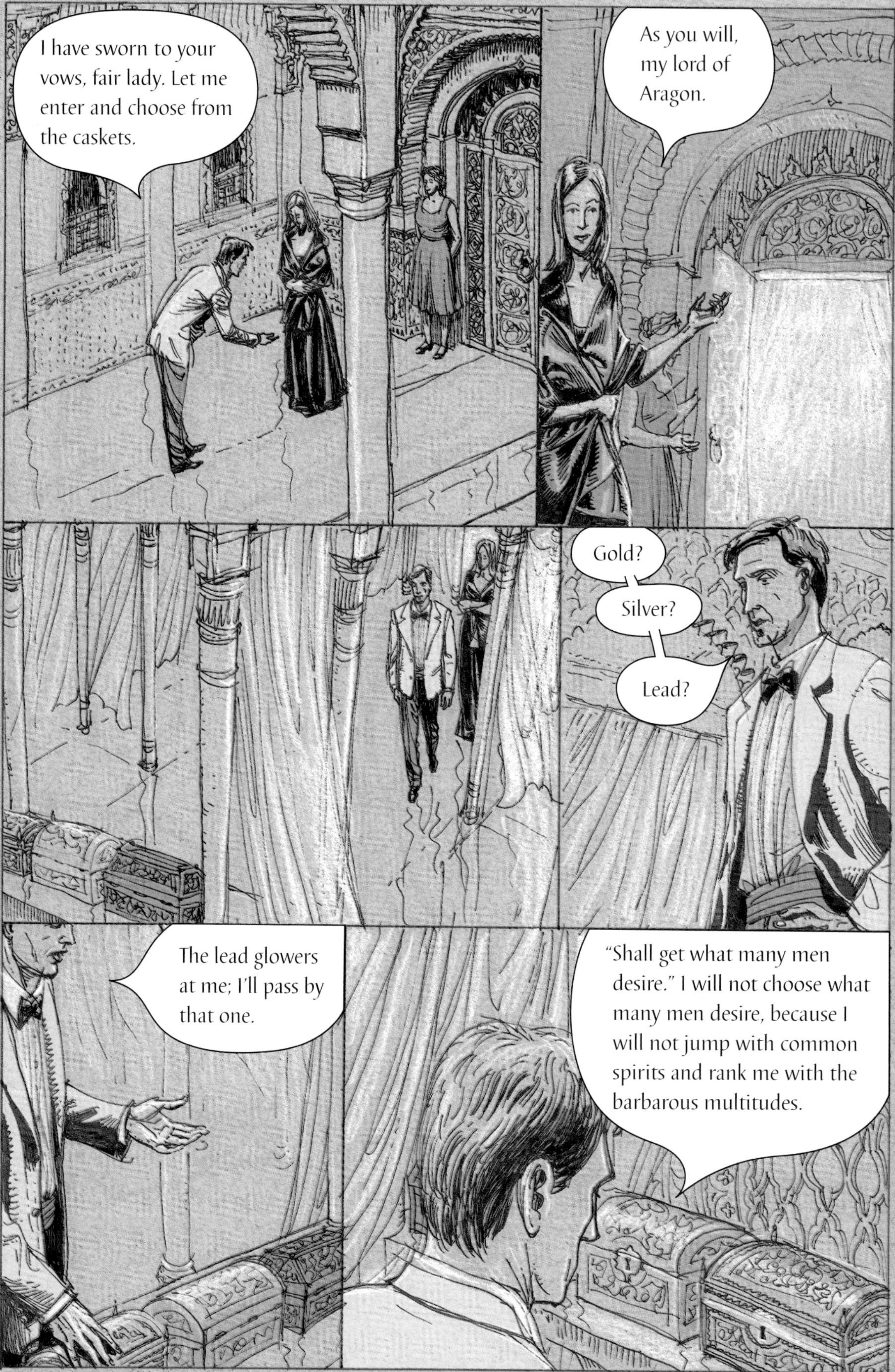
I have sworn to your vows, fair lady. Let me enter and choose from the caskets.
As you will, my lord of Aragon.
Gold?
Silver?
Lead?
The lead glowers at me; I'll pass by that one.
"Shall get what many men desire." I will not choose what many men desire, because I will not jump with common spirits and rank me with the barbarous multitudes.

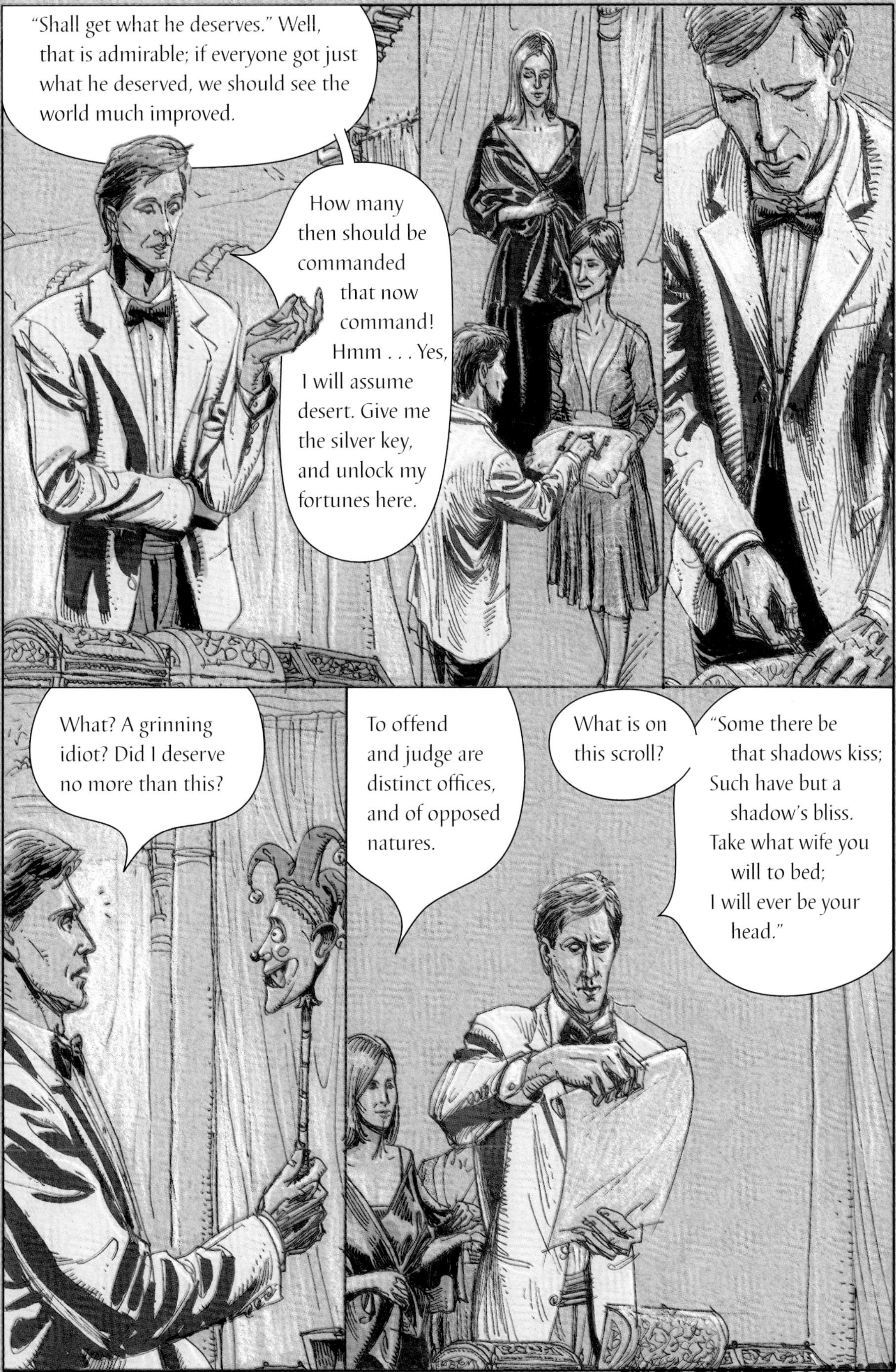
"Shall get what he deserves." Well, that is admirable; if everyone got just what he deserved, we should see the world much improved.
How many then should be commanded that now command! Hmm . . . Yes, I will assume desert. Give me the silver key, and unlock my fortunes here.
What? A grinning idiot? Did I deserve no more than this?
To offend and judge are distinct offices, and of opposed natures.
What is on this scroll?
"Some there be that shadows kiss; Such have but a shadow's bliss. Take what wife you will to bed; I will ever be your head."

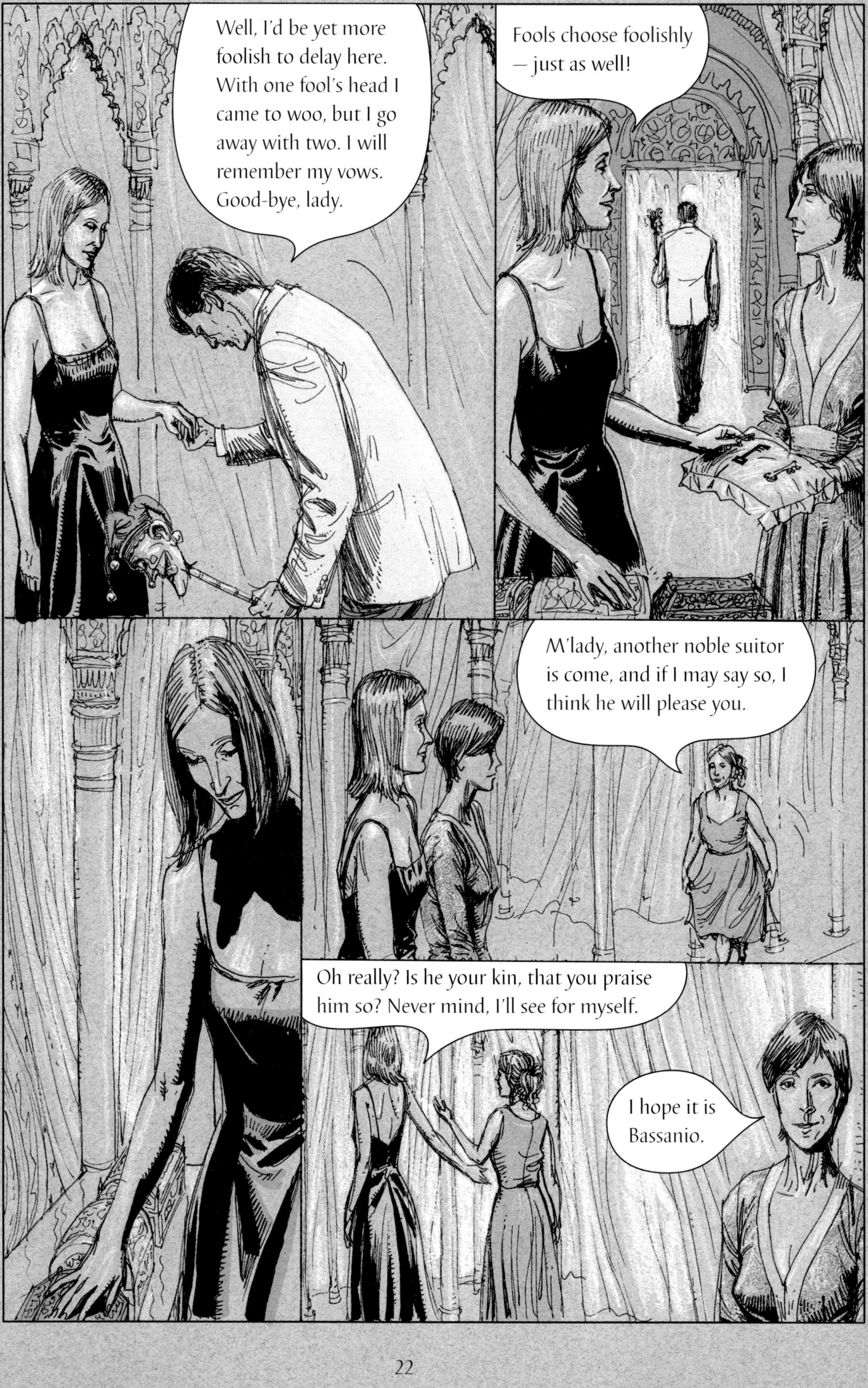
Well, I'd be yet more foolish to delay here. With one fool's head I came to woo, but I go away with two. I will remember my vows. Good-bye, lady.
Fools choose foolishly — just as well!
M'lady, another noble suitor is come, and if I may say so, I think he will please you.
Oh really? Is he your kin, that you praise him so? Never mind, I'll see for myself.
I hope it is Bassanio.

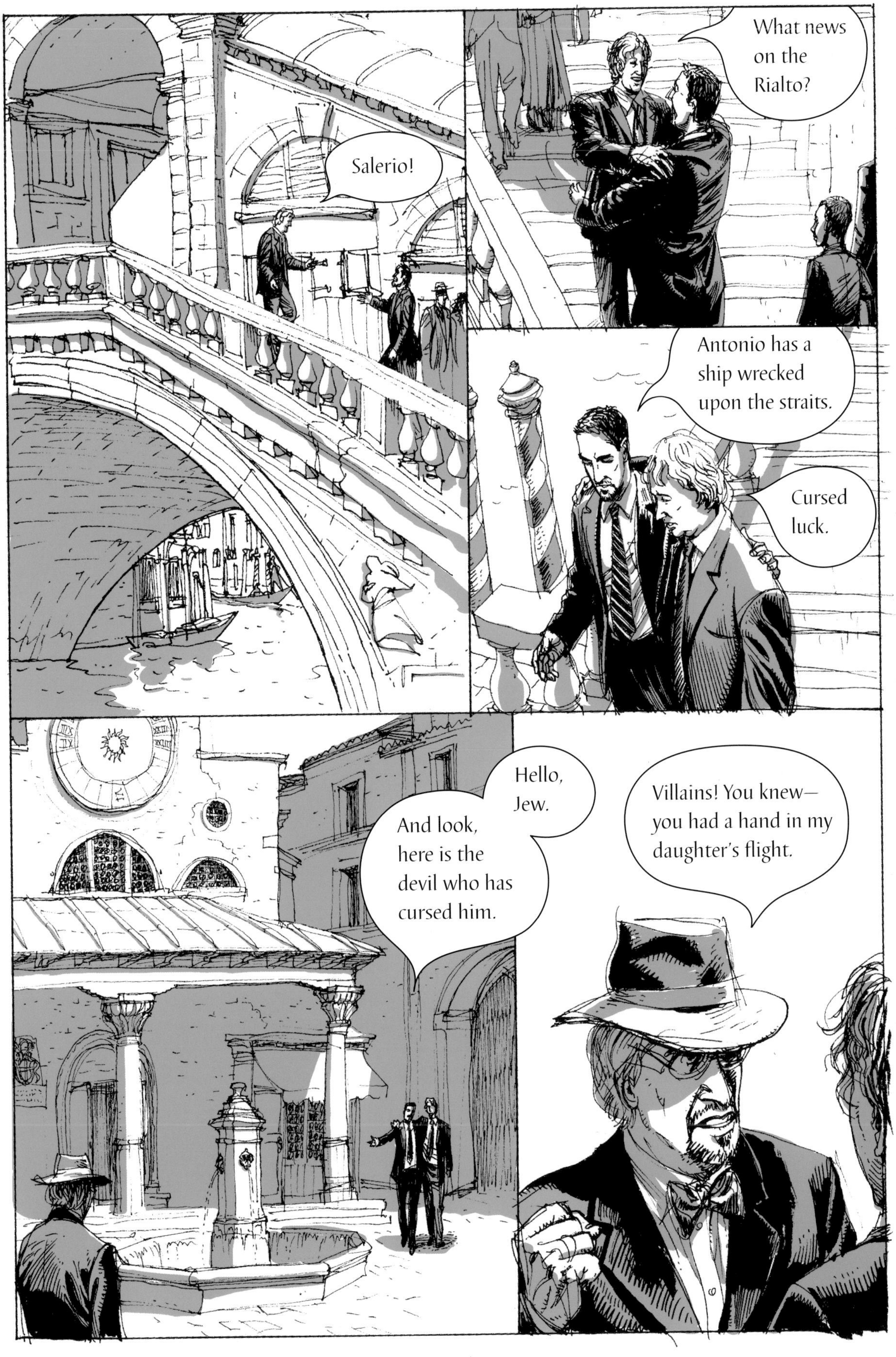
Salerio!
What news on the Rialto?
Antonio has a ship wrecked upon the straits.
Cursed luck.
Hello, Jew.
And look, here is the devil who has cursed him.
Villains! You knew— you had a hand in my daughter's flight.

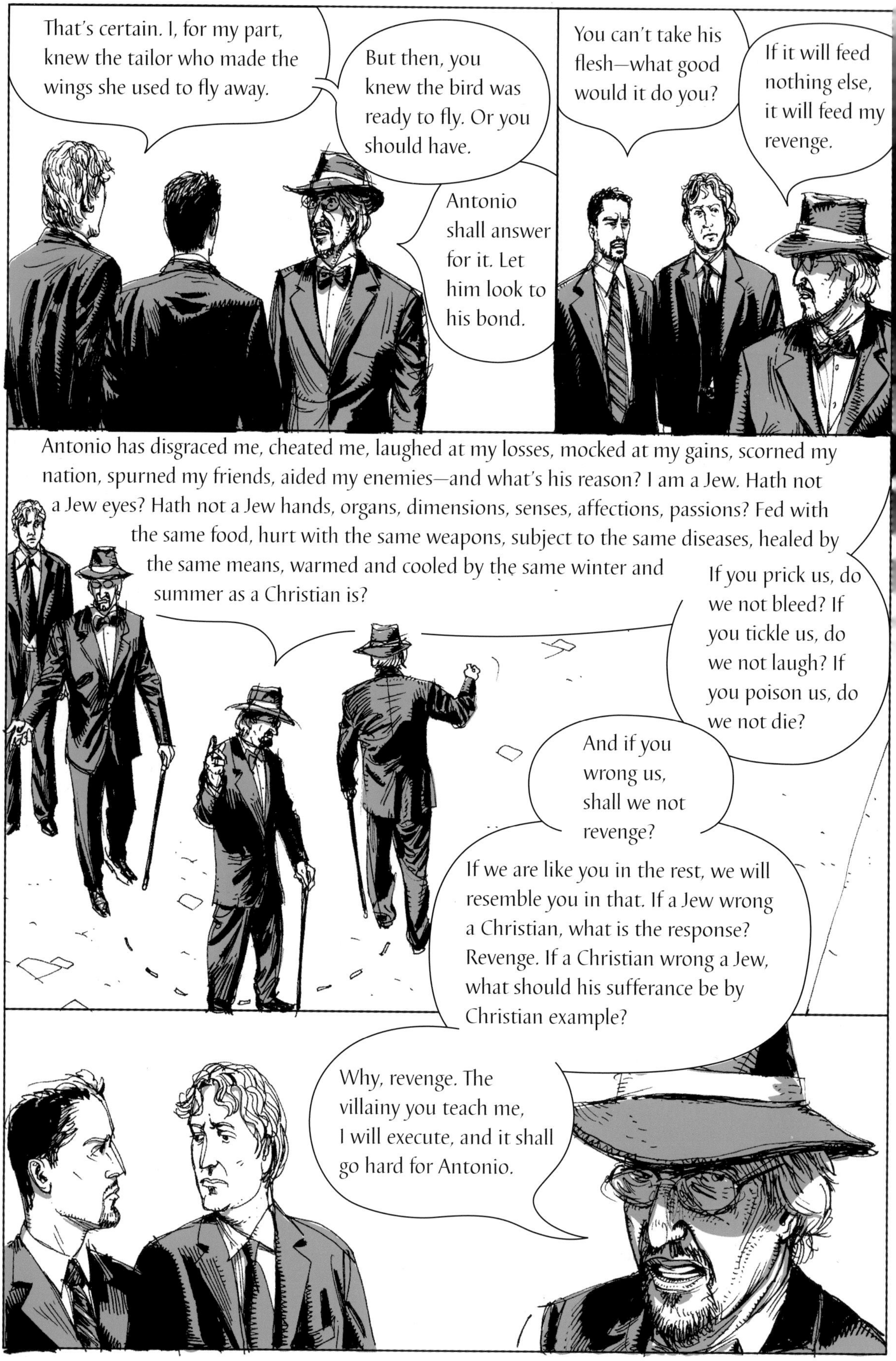
That's certain. I, for my part, knew the tailor who made the wings she used to fly away.
But then, you knew the bird was ready to fly. Or you should have.
Antonio shall answer for it. Let him look to his bond.
You can't take his flesh—what good would it do you?
If it will feed nothing else, it will feed my revenge.
Antonio has disgraced me, cheated me, laughed at my losses, mocked at my gains, scorned my nation, spurned my friends, aided my enemies—and what's his reason? I am a Jew. Hath not a Jew eyes? Hath not a Jew hands, organs, dimensions, senses, affections, passions? Fed with the same food, hurt with the same weapons, subject to the same diseases, healed by the same means, warmed and cooled by the same winter and summer as a Christian is?
If you prick us, do we not bleed? If you tickle us, do we not laugh? If you poison us, do we not die?
And if you wrong us, shall we not revenge?
If we are like you in the rest, we will resemble you in that. If a Jew wrong a Christian, what is the response? Revenge. If a Christian wrong a Jew, what should his sufferance be by Christian example?
Why, revenge. The villainy you teach me, I will execute, and it shall go hard for Antonio.

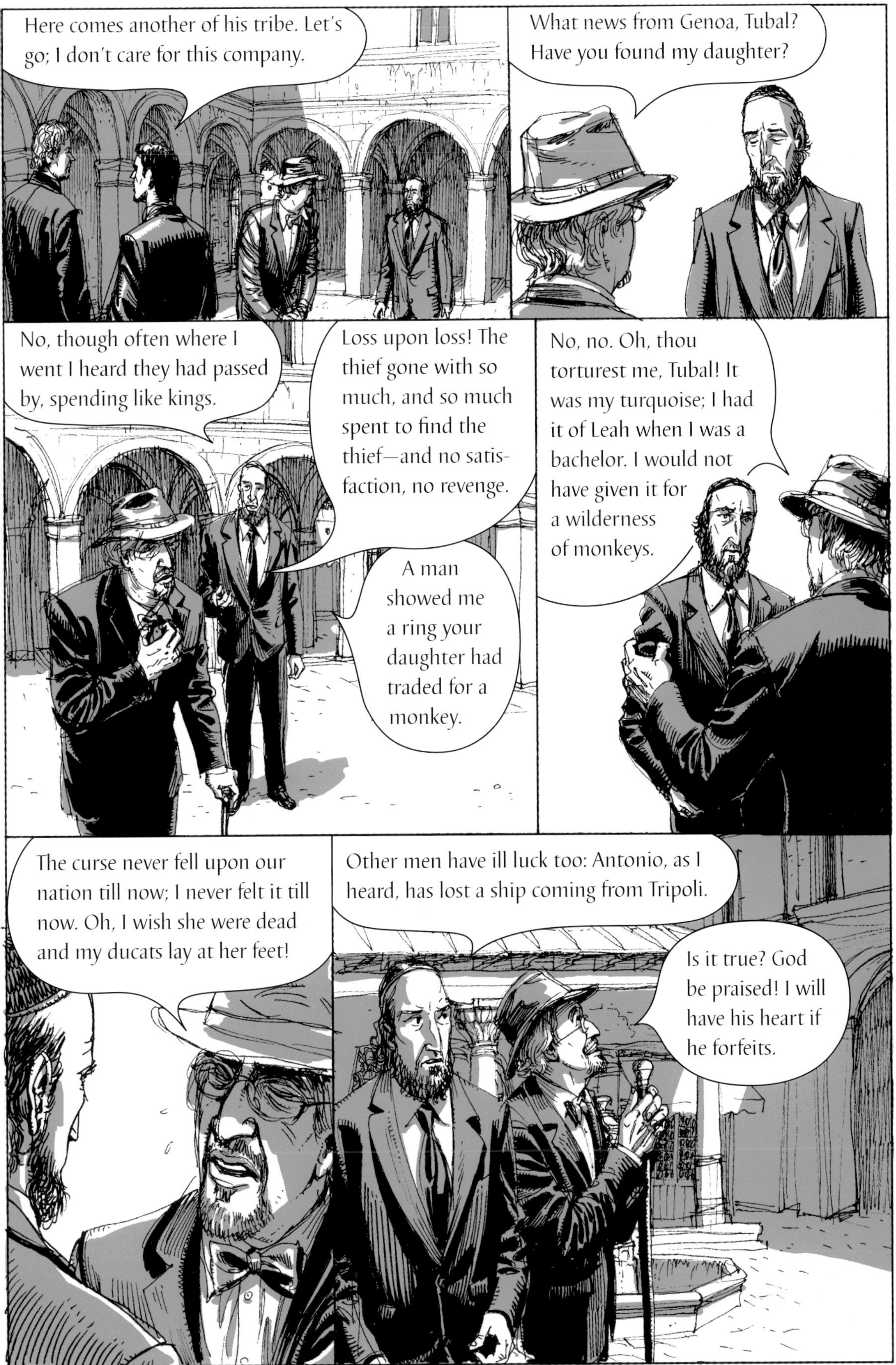
Here comes another of his tribe. Let's go; I don't care for this company.
What news from Genoa, Tubal? Have you found my daughter?
No, though often where I went I heard they had passed by, spending like kings.
Loss upon loss! The thief gone with so much, and so much spent to find the thief—and no satisfaction, no revenge.
A man showed me a ring your daughter had traded for a monkey.
No, no. Oh, thou torturest me, Tubal! It was my turquoise; I had it of Leah when I was a bachelor. I would not have given it for a wilderness of monkeys.
The curse never fell upon our nation till now; I never felt it till now. Oh, I wish she were dead and my ducats lay at her feet!
Other men have ill luck too: Antonio, as I heard, has lost a ship coming from Tripoli.
Is it true? God be praised! I will have his heart if he forfeits.

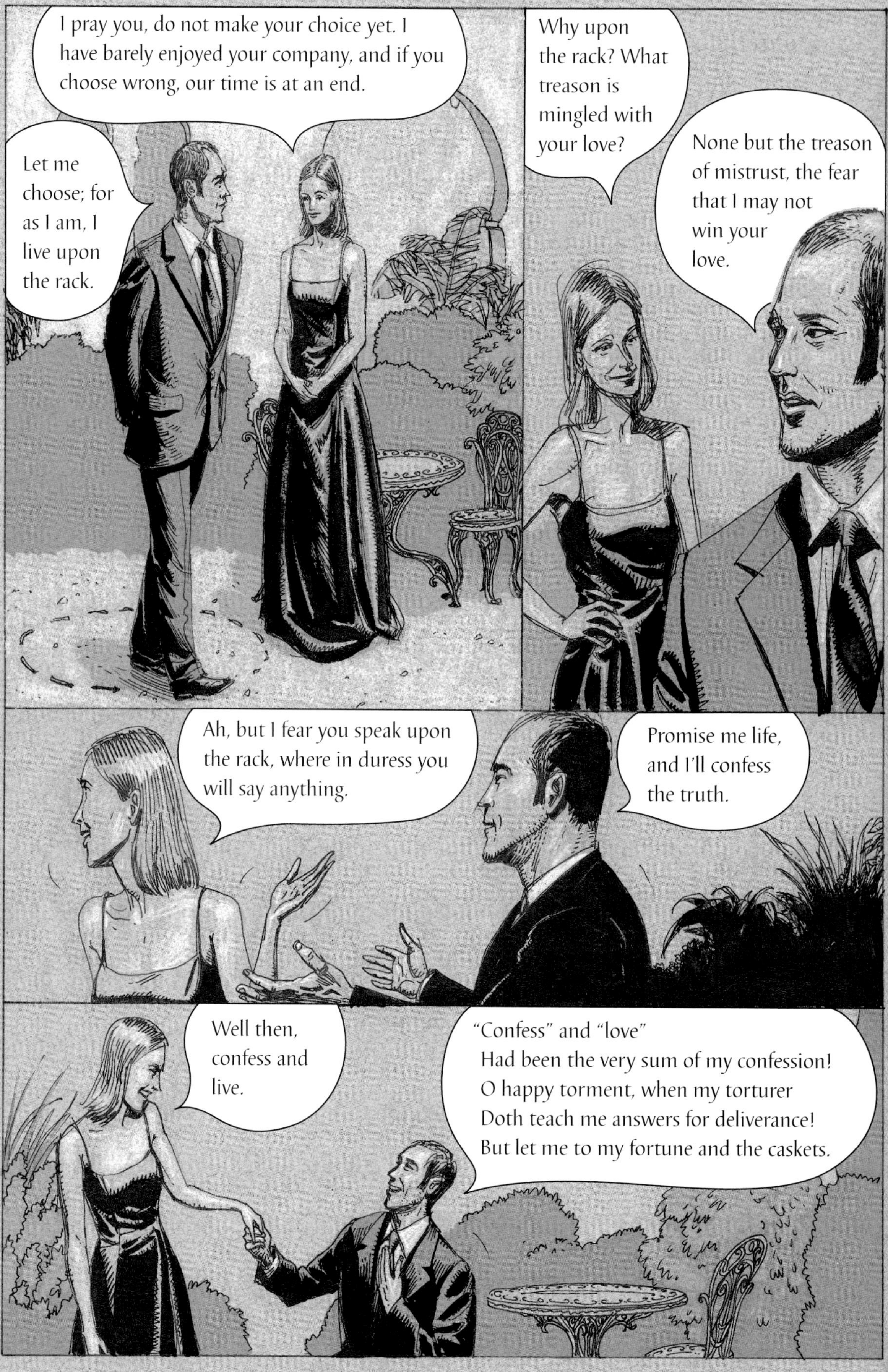
I pray you, do not make your choice yet. I have barely enjoyed your company, and if you choose wrong, our time is at an end.
Let me choose; for as I am, I live upon the rack.
Why upon the rack? What treason is mingled with your love?
None but the treason of mistrust, the fear that I may not win your love.
Ah, but I fear you speak upon the rack, where in duress you will say anything.
Promise me life, and I'll confess the truth.
Well then, confess and live.
"Confess" and "love"
Had been the very sum of my confession!
O happy torment, when my torturer
Doth teach me answers for deliverance!
But let me to my fortune and the caskets.

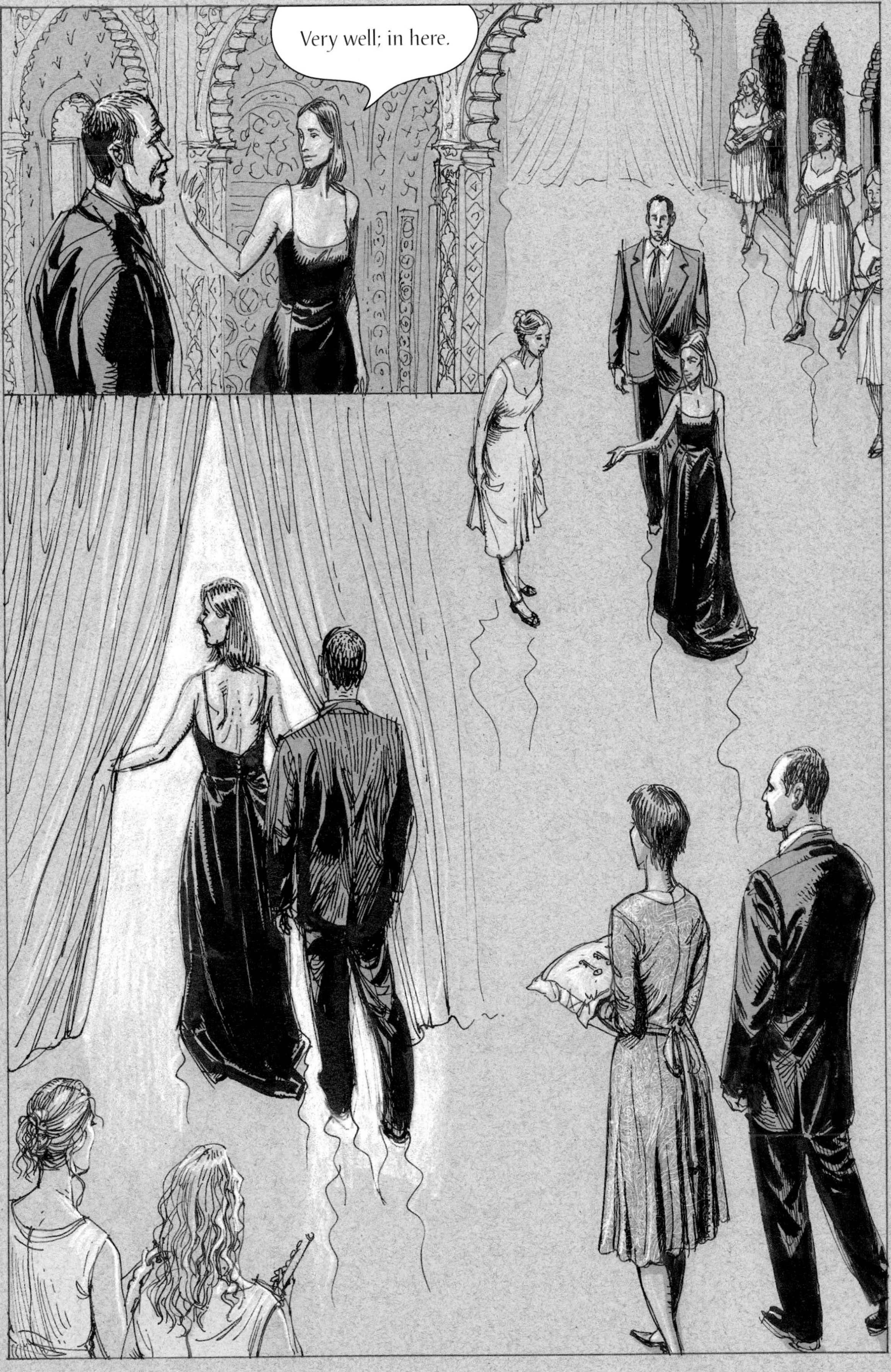

Very well; in here.

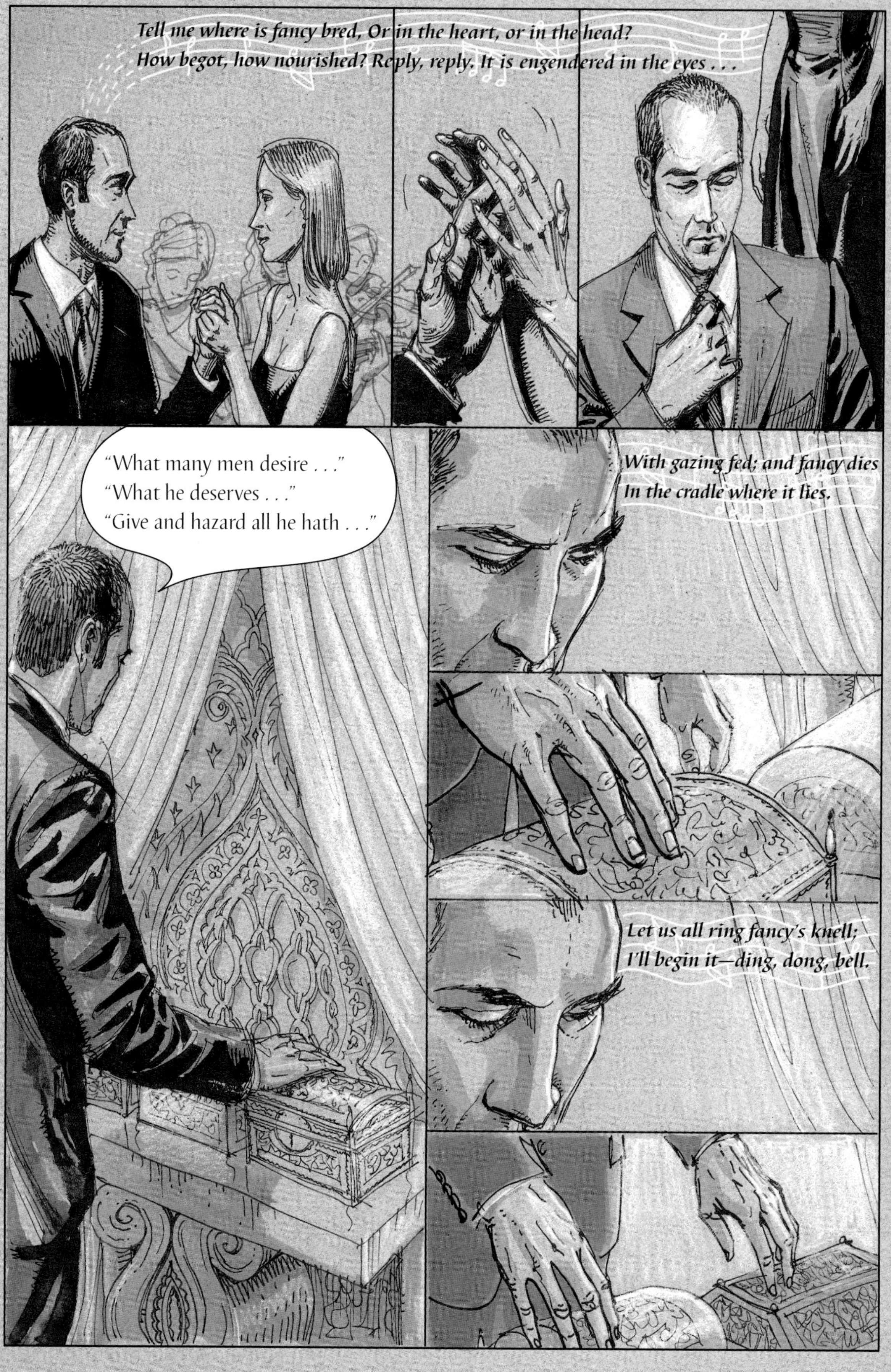
Tell me where is fancy bred, Or in the heart, or in the head?
How begot, how nourished? Reply, reply. It is engendered in the eyes . . .
"What many men desire . . ."
"What he deserves . . ."
"Give and hazard all he hath . . ."
With gazing fed; and fancy dies
In the cradle where it lies.
Let us all ring fancy's knell;
I'll begin it—ding, dong, bell.

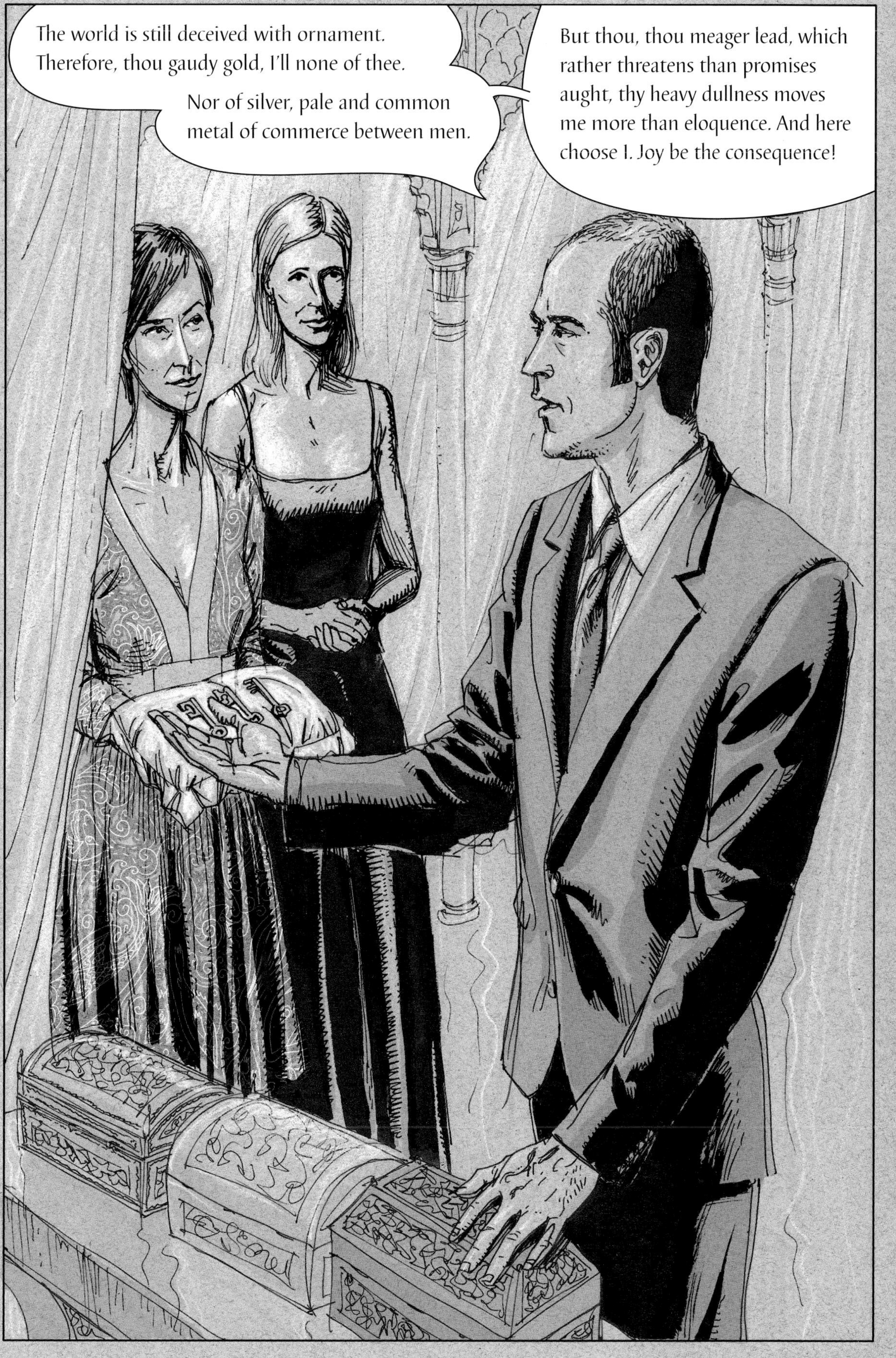
The world is still deceived with ornament. Therefore, thou gaudy gold, I'll none of thee.
Nor of silver, pale and common metal of commerce between men.
But thou, thou meager lead, which rather threatens than promises aught, thy heavy dullness moves me more than eloquence. And here choose I. Joy be the consequence!

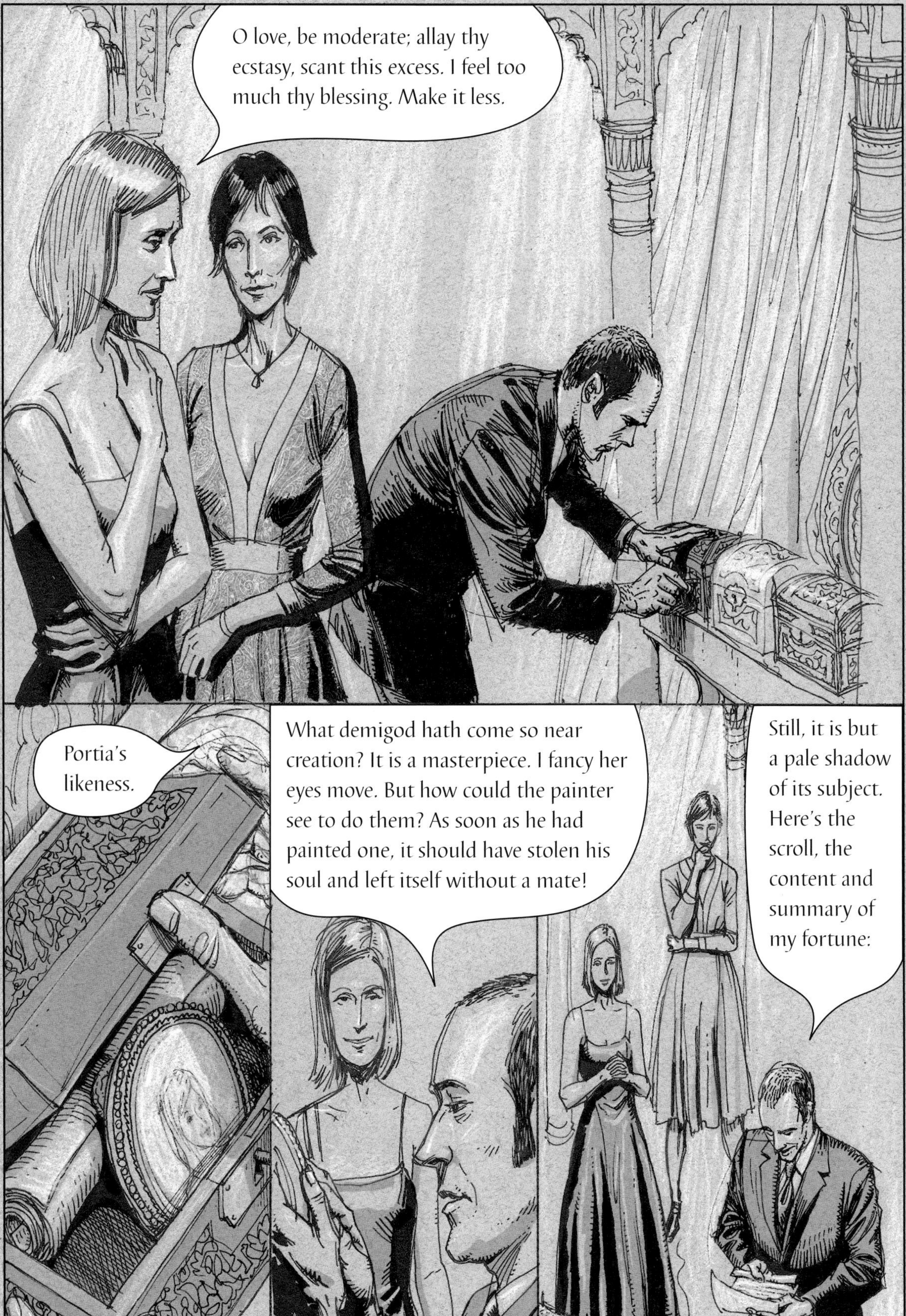
O love, be moderate; allay thy ecstasy, scant this excess. I feel too much thy blessing. Make it less.
Portia's likeness.
What demigod hath come so near creation? It is a masterpiece. I fancy her eyes move. But how could the painter see to do them? As soon as he had painted one, it should have stolen his soul and left itself without a mate!
Still, it is but a pale shadow of its subject. Here's the scroll, the content and summary of my fortune:

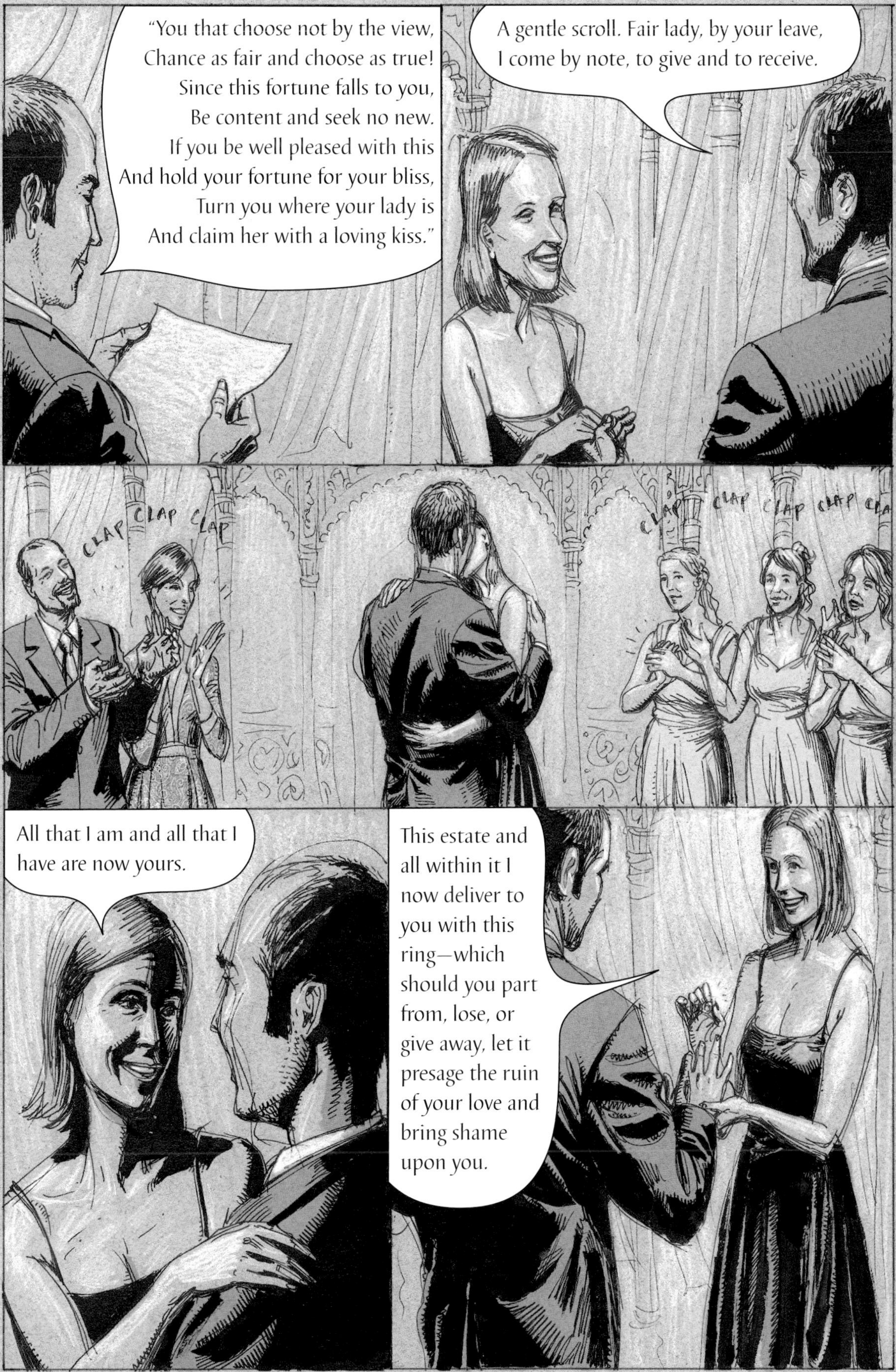
"You that choose not by the view,
Chance as fair and choose as true!
Since this fortune falls to you,
Be content and seek no new.
If you be well pleased with this
And hold your fortune for your bliss,
Turn you where your lady is
And claim her with a loving kiss."
A gentle scroll. Fair lady, by your leave,
I come by note, to give and to receive.
CLAP CLAP CLAP
CLAP CLAP CLAP CLAP CLA
All that I am and all that I have are now yours.
This estate and all within it I now deliver to you with this ring—which should you part from, lose, or give away, let it presage the ruin of your love and bring shame upon you.

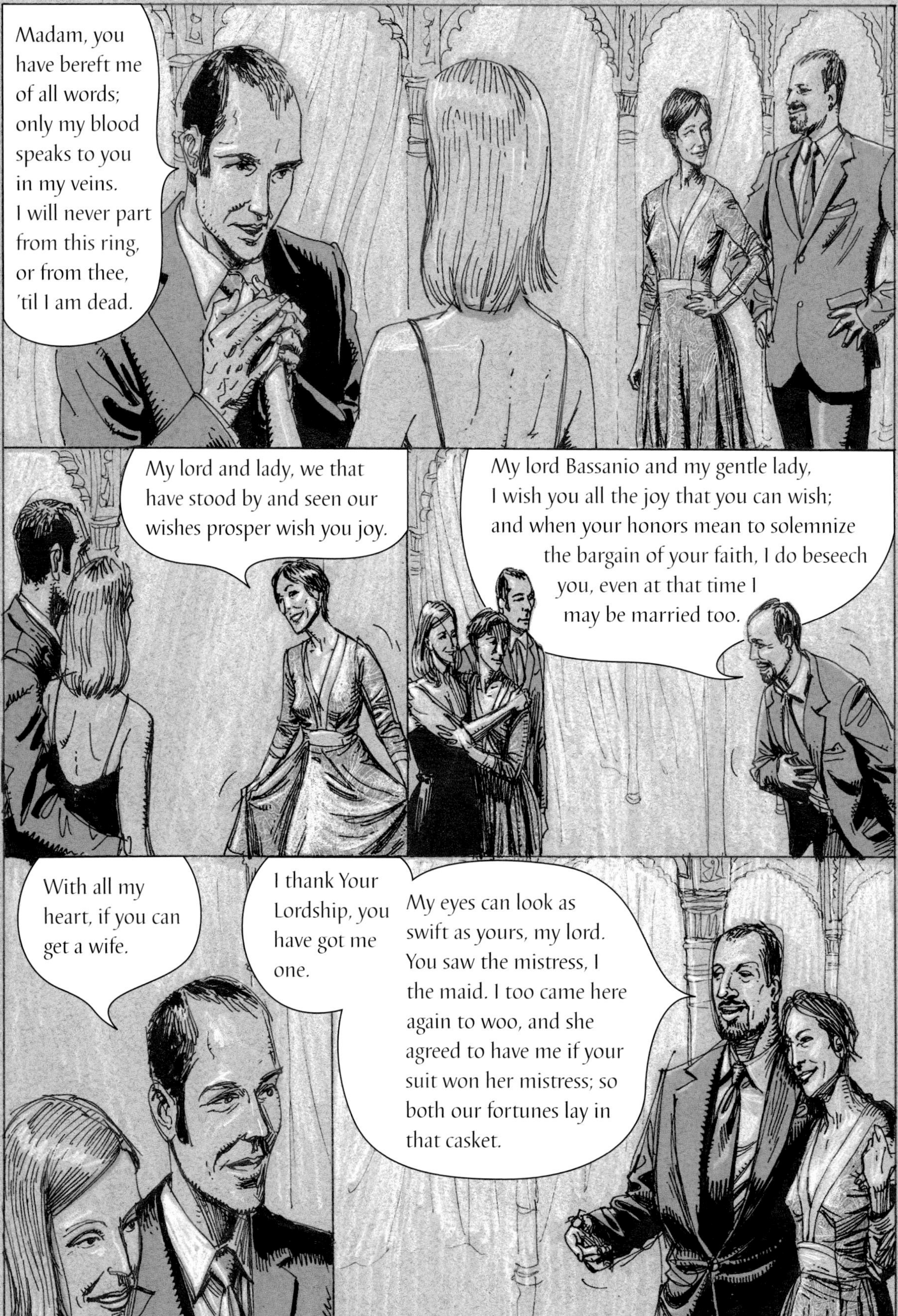
Madam, you have bereft me of all words; only my blood speaks to you in my veins. I will never part from this ring, or from thee, 'til I am dead.
My lord and lady, we that have stood by and seen our wishes prosper wish you joy.
My lord Bassanio and my gentle lady, I wish you all the joy that you can wish; and when your honors mean to solemnize the bargain of your faith, I do beseech you, even at that time I may be married too.
With all my heart, if you can get a wife.
I thank Your Lordship, you have got me one.
My eyes can look as swift as yours, my lord. You saw the mistress, I the maid. I too came here again to woo, and she agreed to have me if your suit won her mistress; so both our fortunes lay in that casket.

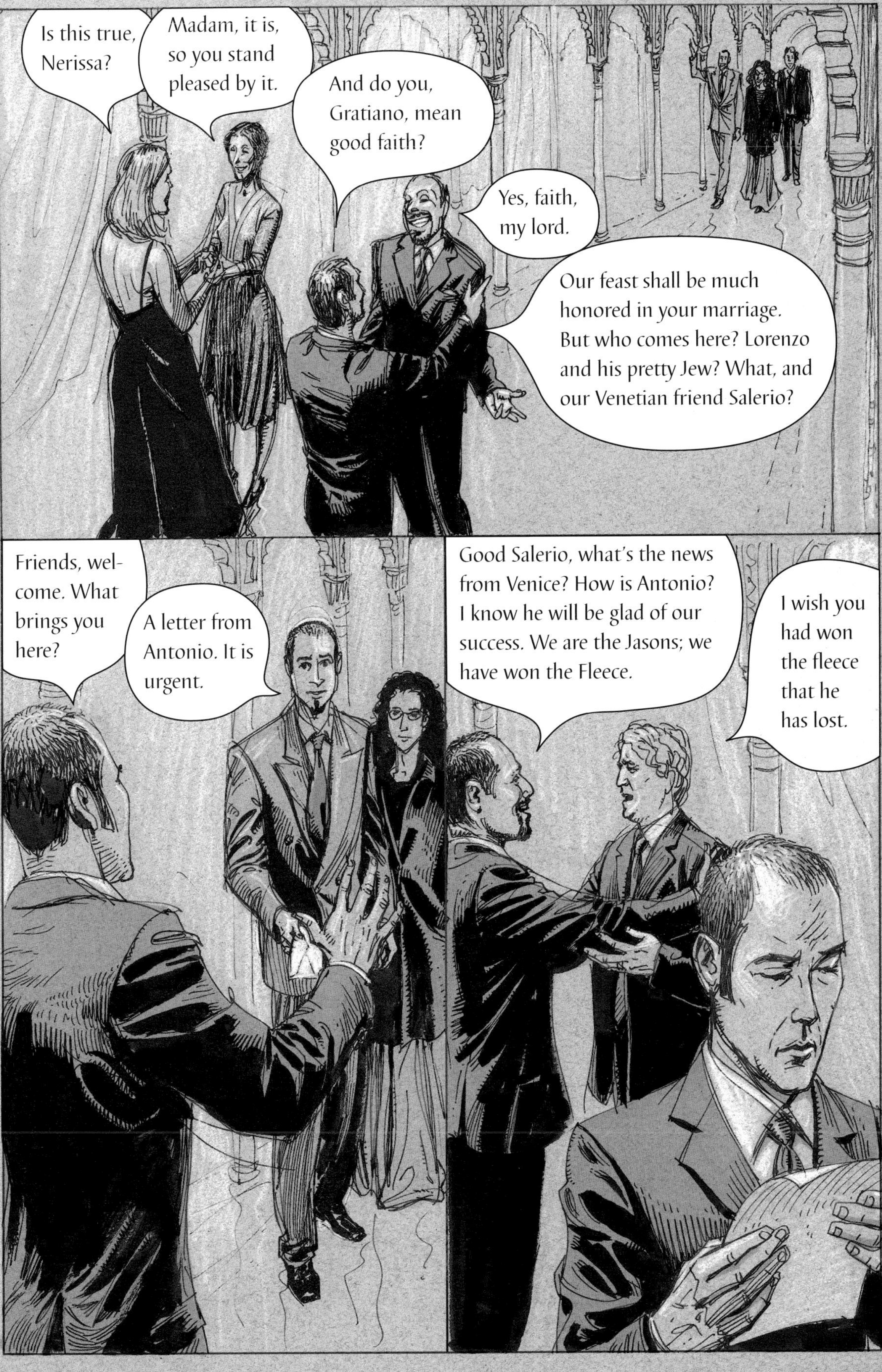
Is this true, Nerissa?
Madam, it is, so you stand pleased by it.
And do you, Gratiano, mean good faith?
Yes, faith, my lord.
Our feast shall be much honored in your marriage. But who comes here? Lorenzo and his pretty Jew? What, and our Venetian friend Salerio?
Friends, wel-come. What brings you here?
A letter from Antonio. It is urgent.
Good Salerio, what's the news from Venice? How is Antonio? I know he will be glad of our success. We are the Jasons; we have won the Fleece.
I wish you had won the fleece that he has lost.

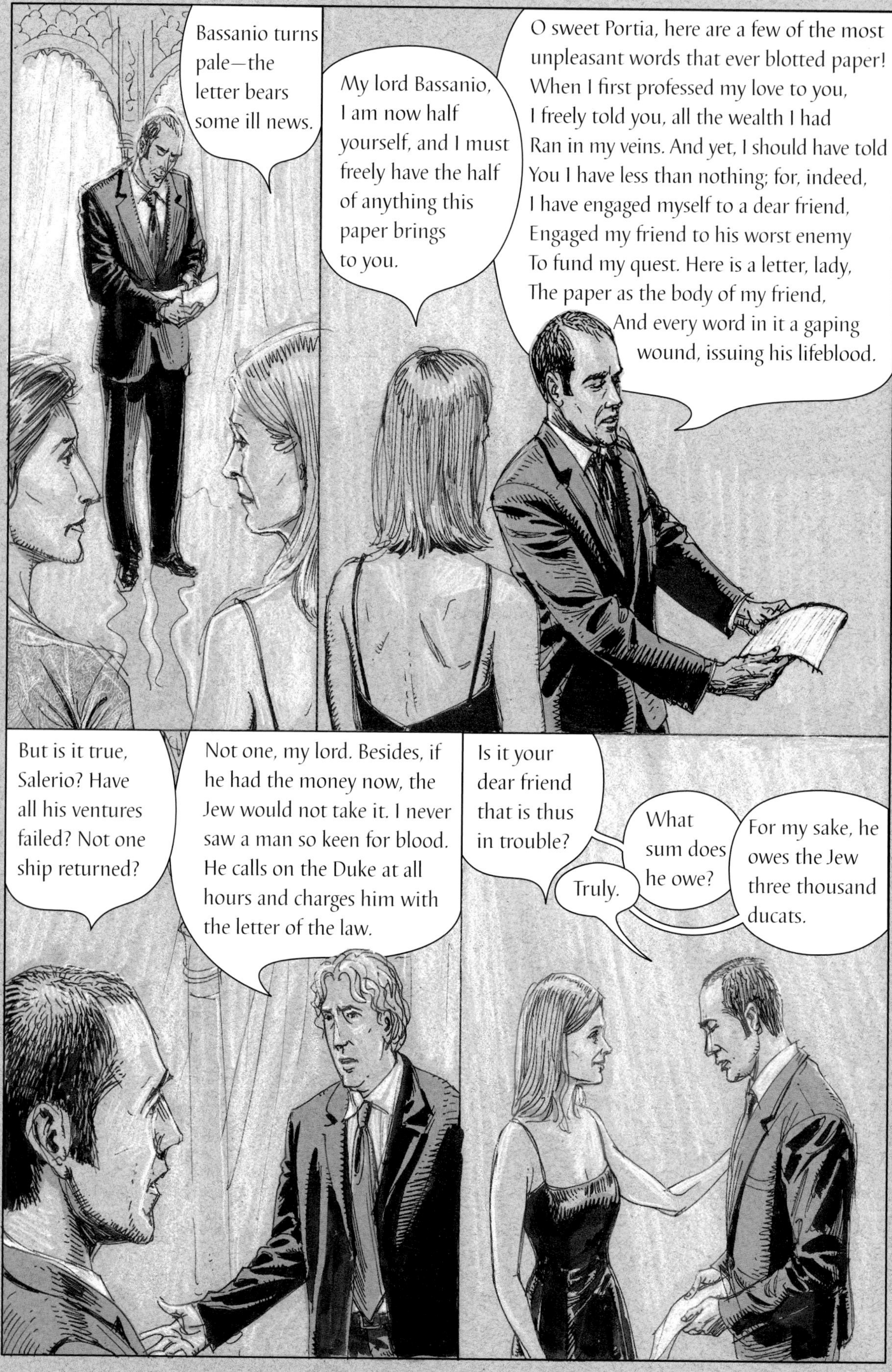
Bassanio turns pale—the letter bears some ill news.
My lord Bassanio, I am now half yourself, and I must freely have the half of anything this paper brings to you.
O sweet Portia, here are a few of the most unpleasant words that ever blotted paper! When I first professed my love to you, I freely told you, all the wealth I had Ran in my veins. And yet, I should have told You I have less than nothing; for, indeed, I have engaged myself to a dear friend, Engaged my friend to his worst enemy To fund my quest. Here is a letter, lady, The paper as the body of my friend, And every word in it a gaping wound, issuing his lifeblood.
But is it true, Salerio? Have all his ventures failed? Not one ship returned?
Not one, my lord. Besides, if he had the money now, the Jew would not take it. I never saw a man so keen for blood. He calls on the Duke at all hours and charges him with the letter of the law.
Is it your dear friend that is thus in trouble?
Truly.
What sum does he owe?
For my sake, he owes the Jew three thousand ducats.

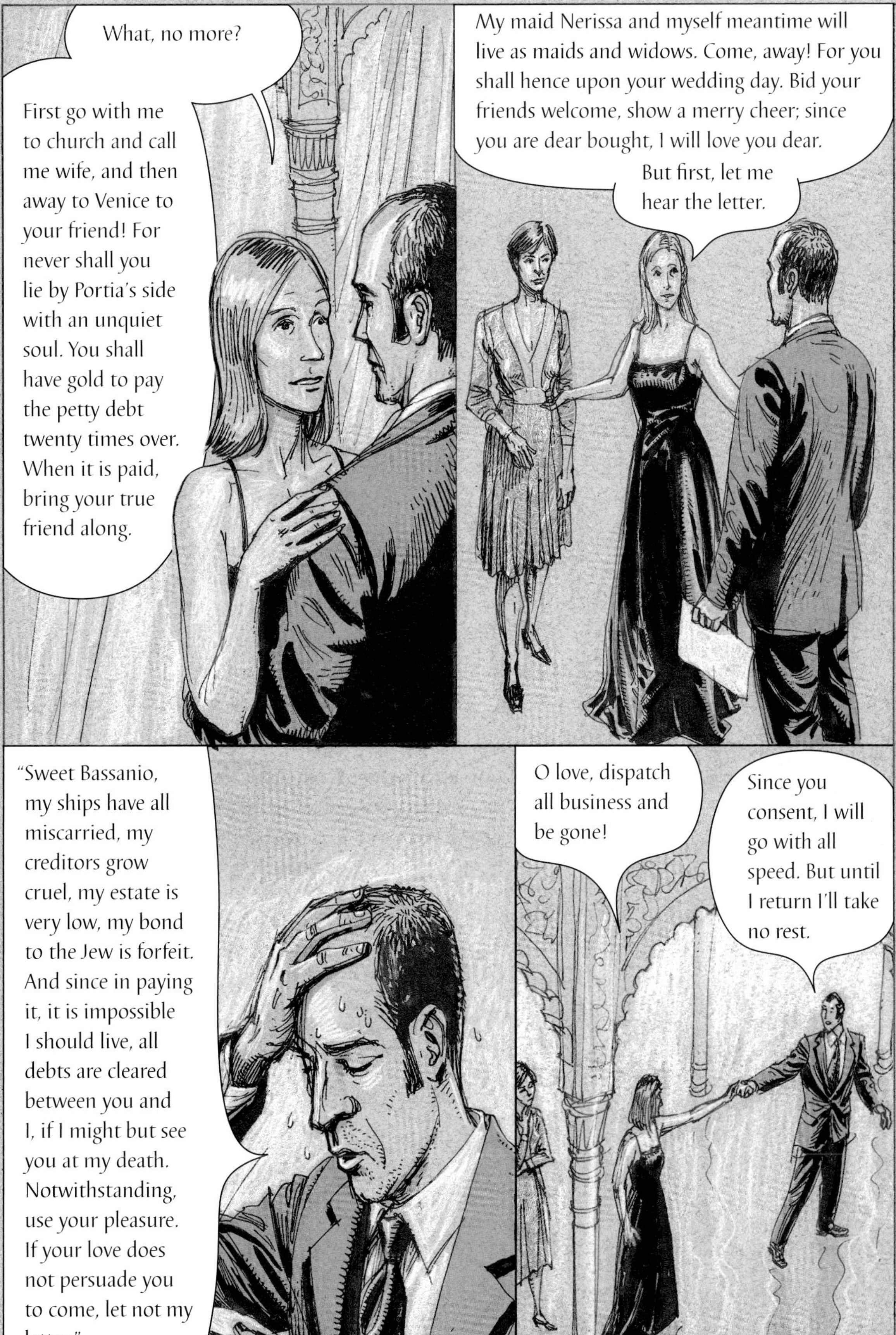
What, no more?
First go with me to church and call me wife, and then away to Venice to your friend! For never shall you lie by Portia's side with an unquiet soul. You shall have gold to pay the petty debt twenty times over. When it is paid, bring your true friend along.
My maid Nerissa and myself meantime will live as maids and widows. Come, away! For you shall hence upon your wedding day. Bid your friends welcome, show a merry cheer; since you are dear bought, I will love you dear.
But first, let me hear the letter.
"Sweet Bassanio, my ships have all miscarried, my creditors grow cruel, my estate is very low, my bond to the Jew is forfeit. And since in paying it, it is impossible I should live, all debts are cleared between you and I, if I might but see you at my death. Notwithstanding, use your pleasure. If your love does not persuade you to come, let not my letter."
O love, dispatch all business and be gone!
Since you consent, I will go with all speed. But until I return I'll take no rest.

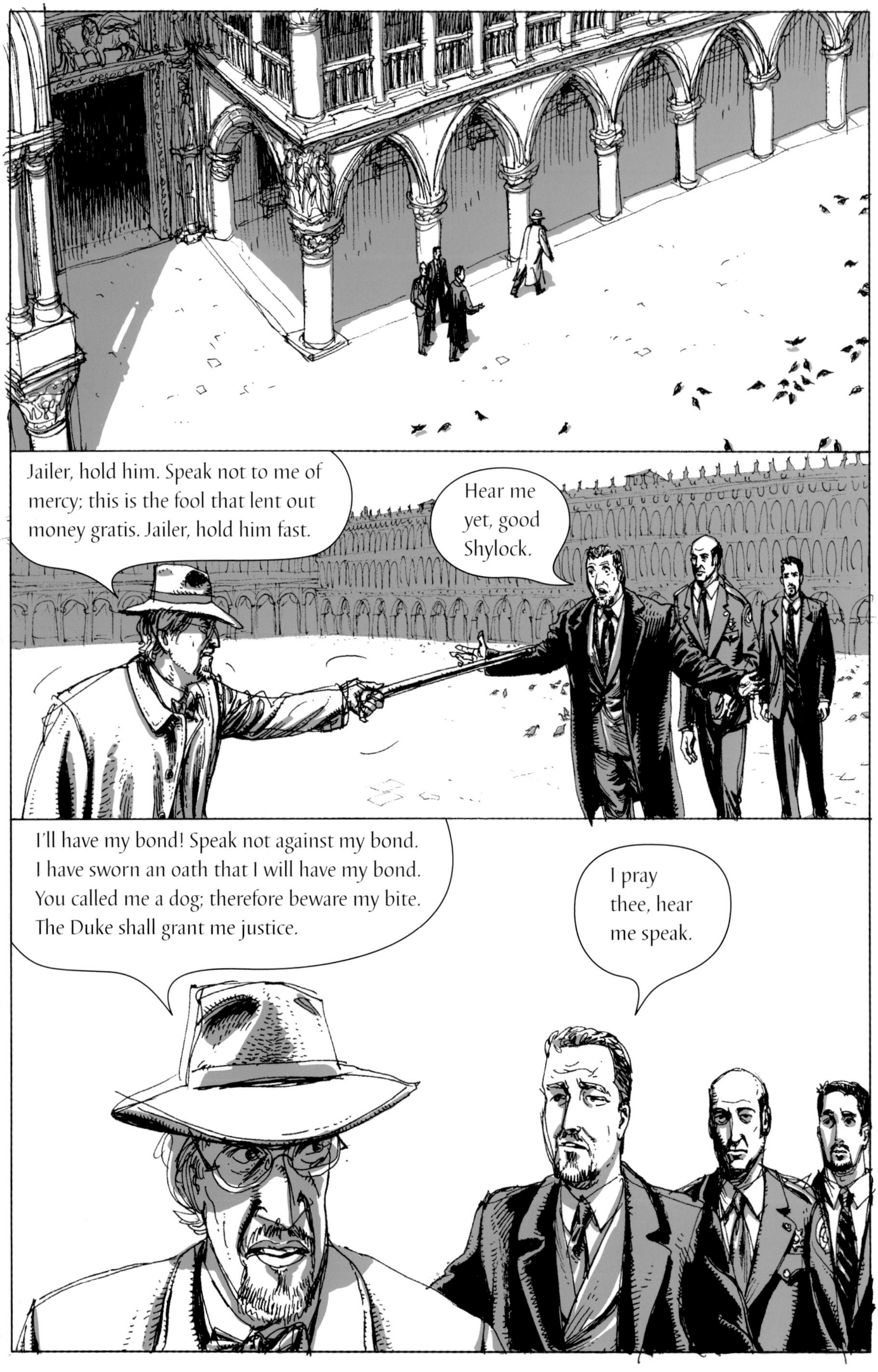
Jailer, hold him. Speak not to me of mercy; this is the fool that lent out money gratis. Jailer, hold him fast.
Hear me yet, good Shylock.
I'll have my bond! Speak not against my bond. I have sworn an oath that I will have my bond. You called me a dog; therefore beware my bite. The Duke shall grant me justice.
I pray thee, hear me speak.

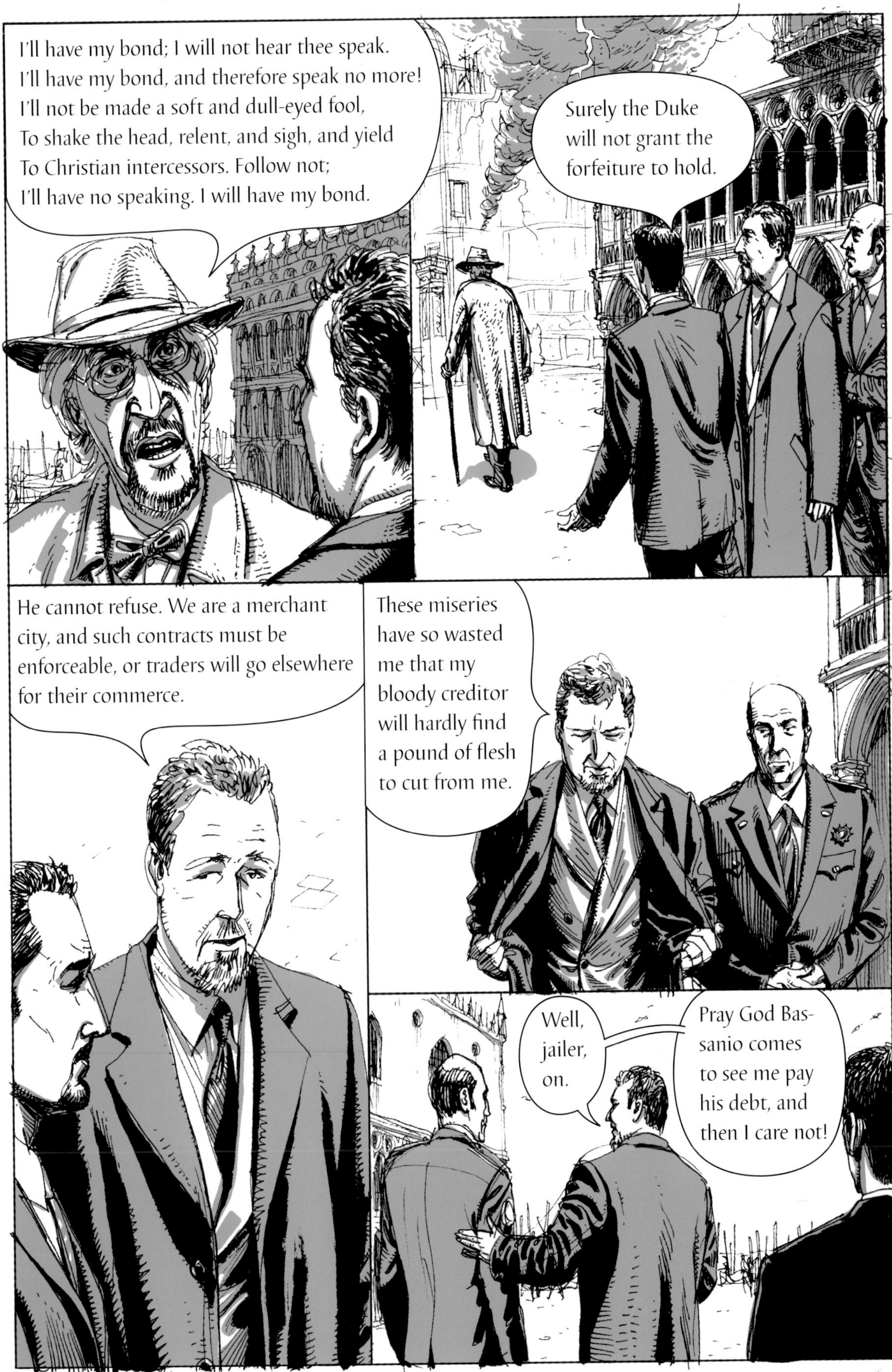
I'll have my bond; I will not hear thee speak.
I'll have my bond, and therefore speak no more!
I'll not be made a soft and dull-eyed fool,
To shake the head, relent, and sigh, and yield
To Christian intercessors. Follow not;
I'll have no speaking. I will have my bond.
Surely the Duke will not grant the forfeiture to hold.
He cannot refuse. We are a merchant city, and such contracts must be enforceable, or traders will go elsewhere for their commerce.
These miseries have so wasted me that my bloody creditor will hardly find a pound of flesh to cut from me.
Well, jailer, on.
Pray God Bassanio comes to see me pay his debt, and then I care not!

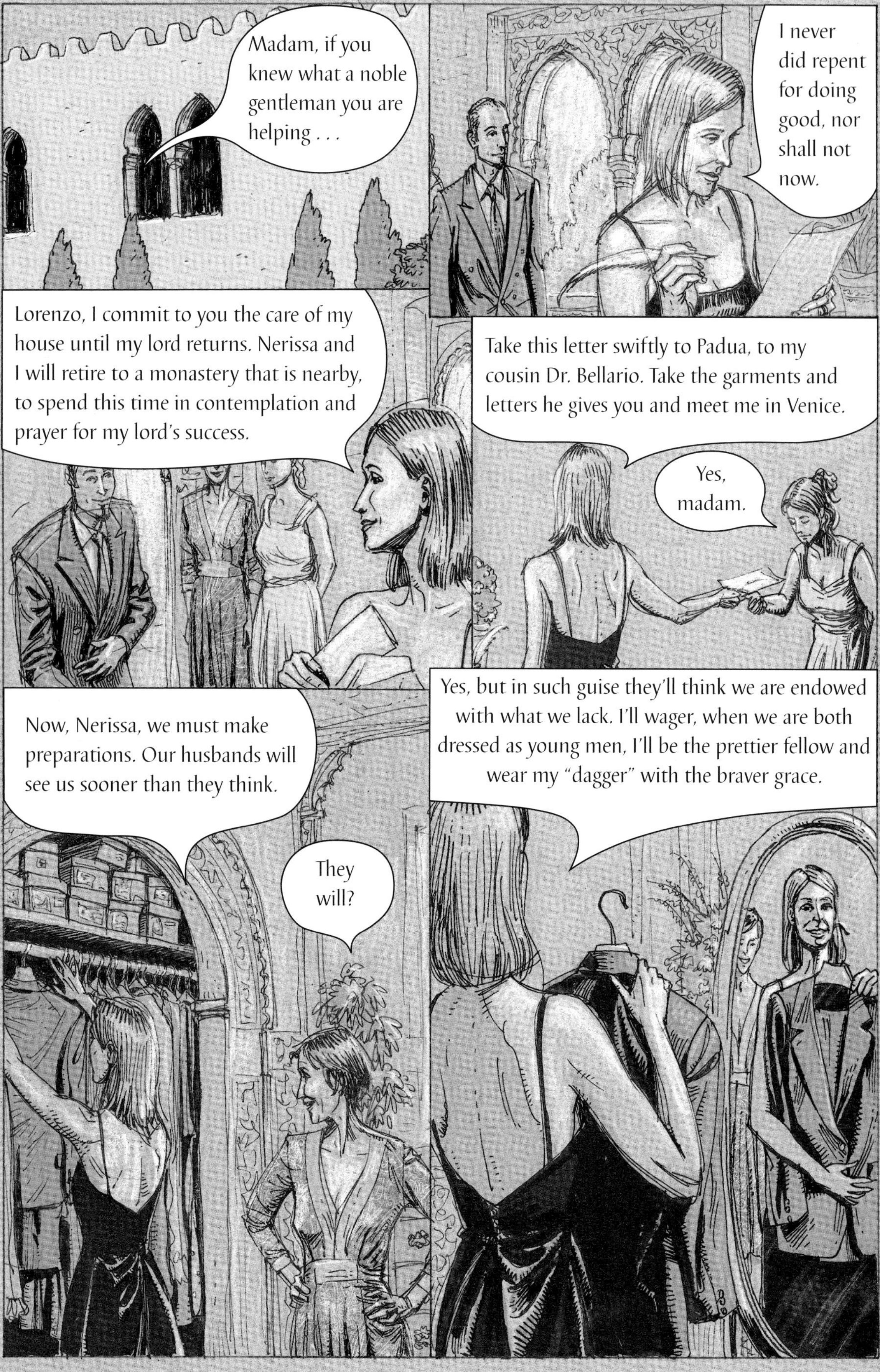
Madam, if you knew what a noble gentleman you are helping . . .
I never did repent for doing good, nor shall not now.
Lorenzo, I commit to you the care of my house until my lord returns. Nerissa and I will retire to a monastery that is nearby, to spend this time in contemplation and prayer for my lord's success.
Take this letter swiftly to Padua, to my cousin Dr. Bellario. Take the garments and letters he gives you and meet me in Venice.
Yes, madam.
Now, Nerissa, we must make preparations. Our husbands will see us sooner than they think.
They will?
Yes, but in such guise they'll think we are endowed with what we lack. I'll wager, when we are both dressed as young men, I'll be the prettier fellow and wear my "dagger" with the braver grace.

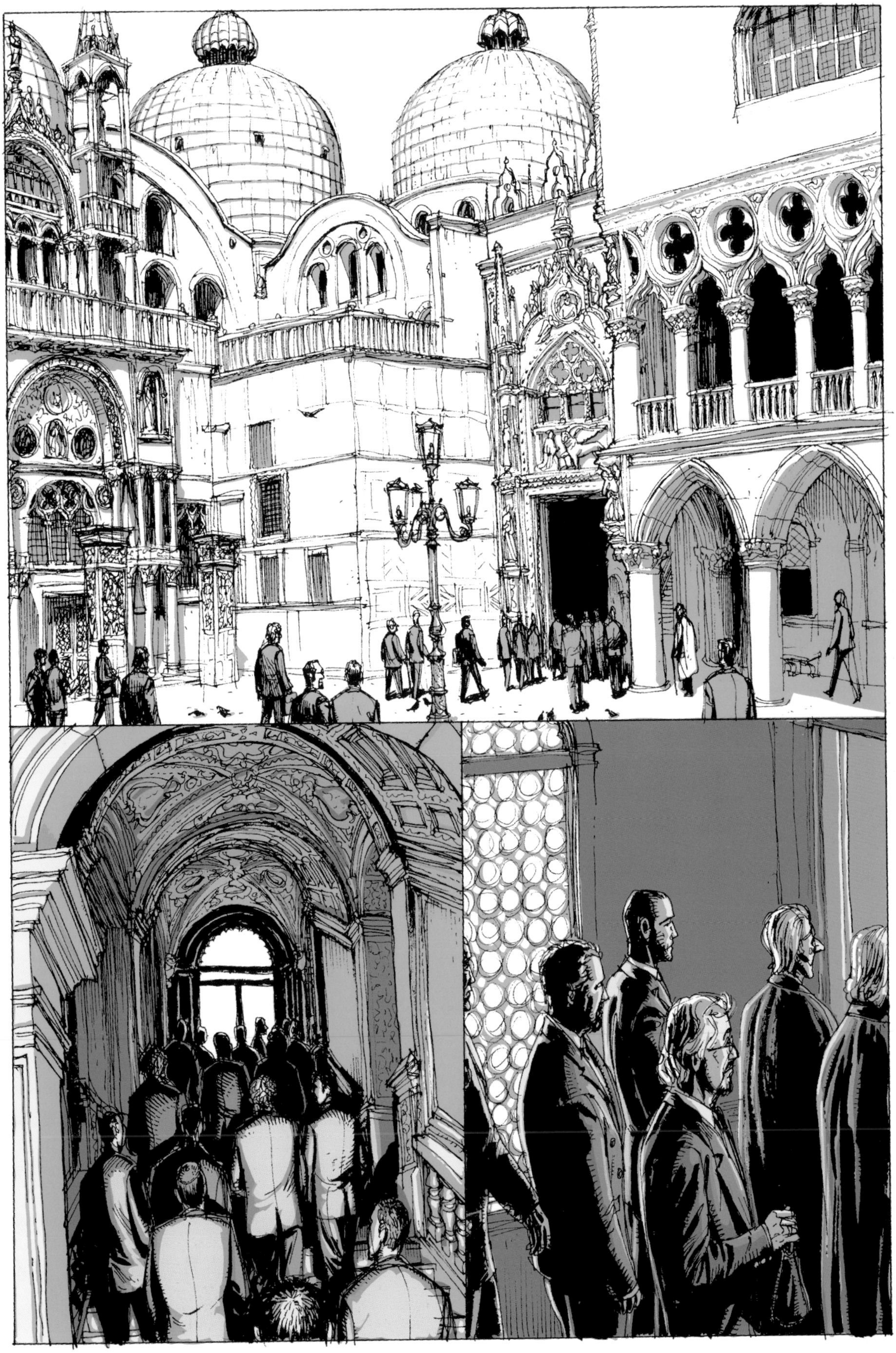

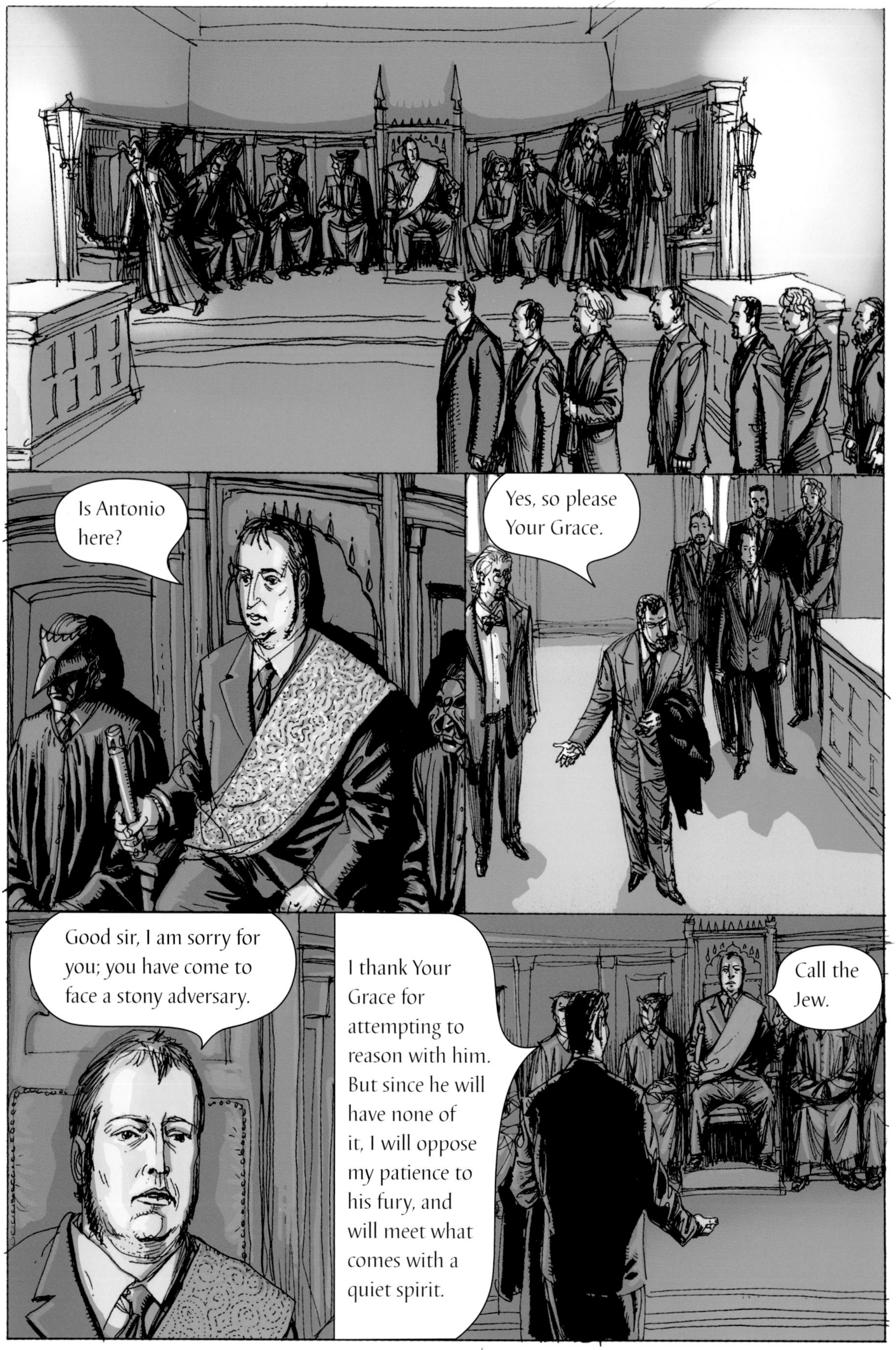
Is Antonio here?
Yes, so please Your Grace.
Good sir, I am sorry for you; you have come to face a stony adversary.
I thank Your Grace for attempting to reason with him. But since he will have none of it, I will oppose my patience to his fury, and will meet what comes with a quiet spirit.
Call the Jew.

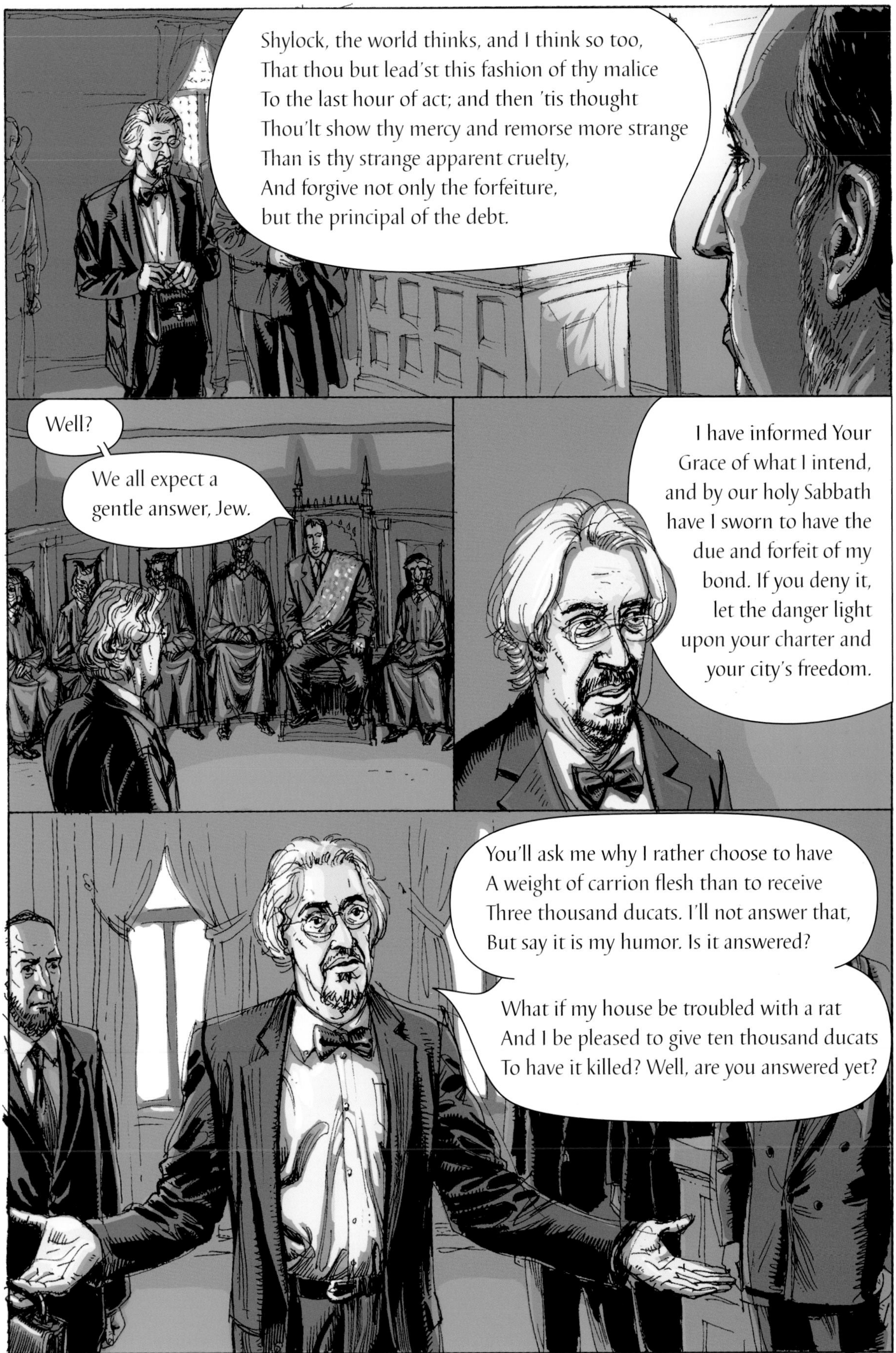
Shylock, the world thinks, and I think so too,
That thou but lead'st this fashion of thy malice
To the last hour of act; and then 'tis thought
Thou'lt show thy mercy and remorse more strange
Than is thy strange apparent cruelty,
And forgive not only the forfeiture,
but the principal of the debt.
Well?
We all expect a gentle answer, Jew.
I have informed Your Grace of what I intend, and by our holy Sabbath have I sworn to have the due and forfeit of my bond. If you deny it, let the danger light upon your charter and your city's freedom.
You'll ask me why I rather choose to have
A weight of carrion flesh than to receive
Three thousand ducats. I'll not answer that,
But say it is my humor. Is it answered?
What if my house be troubled with a rat
And I be pleased to give ten thousand ducats
To have it killed? Well, are you answered yet?

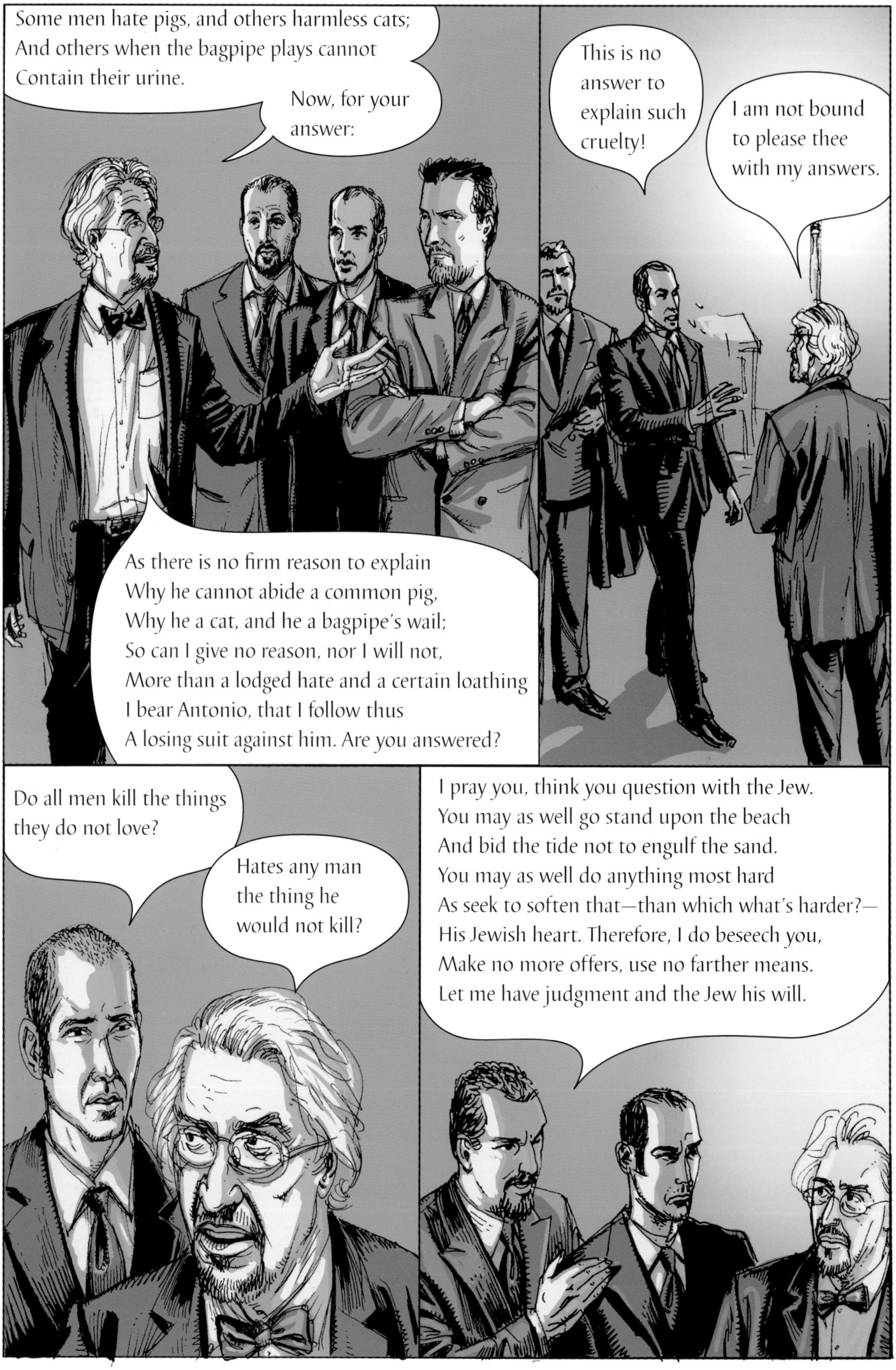
Some men hate pigs, and others harmless cats; And others when the bagpipe plays cannot Contain their urine.
Now, for your answer:
As there is no firm reason to explain Why he cannot abide a common pig, Why he a cat, and he a bagpipe's wail; So can I give no reason, nor I will not, More than a lodged hate and a certain loathing I bear Antonio, that I follow thus A losing suit against him. Are you answered?
This is no answer to explain such cruelty!
I am not bound to please thee with my answers.
Do all men kill the things they do not love?
Hates any man the thing he would not kill?
I pray you, think you question with the Jew. You may as well go stand upon the beach And bid the tide not to engulf the sand. You may as well do anything most hard As seek to soften that—than which what's harder?— His Jewish heart. Therefore, I do beseech you, Make no more offers, use no farther means. Let me have judgment and the Jew his will.

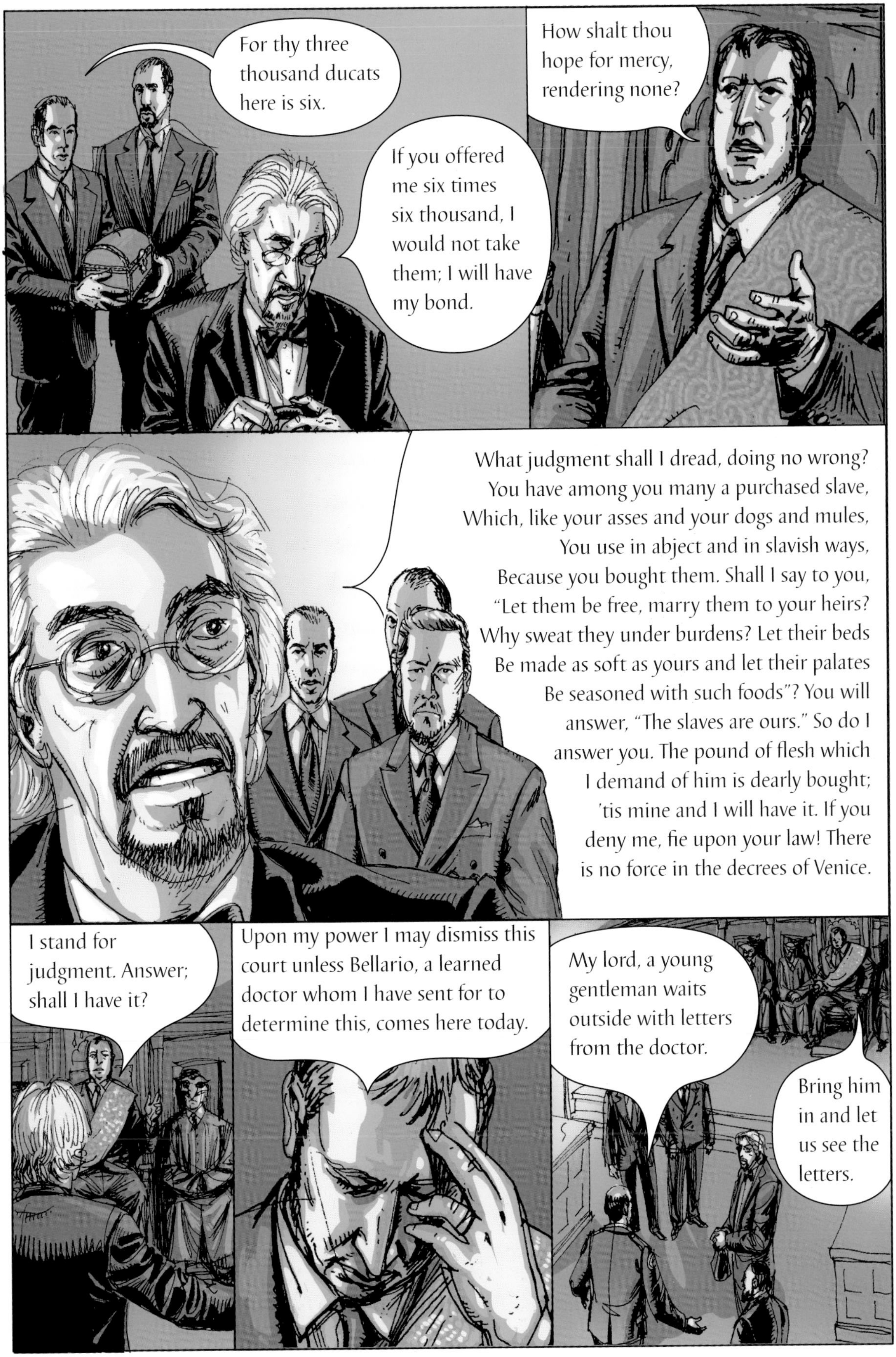
For thy three thousand ducats here is six.
If you offered me six times six thousand, I would not take them; I will have my bond.
How shalt thou hope for mercy, rendering none?
What judgment shall I dread, doing no wrong? You have among you many a purchased slave, Which, like your asses and your dogs and mules, You use in abject and in slavish ways, Because you bought them. Shall I say to you, "Let them be free, marry them to your heirs? Why sweat they under burdens? Let their beds Be made as soft as yours and let their palates Be seasoned with such foods"? You will answer, "The slaves are ours." So do I answer you. The pound of flesh which I demand of him is dearly bought; 'tis mine and I will have it. If you deny me, fie upon your law! There is no force in the decrees of Venice.
I stand for judgment. Answer; shall I have it?
Upon my power I may dismiss this court unless Bellario, a learned doctor whom I have sent for to determine this, comes here today.
My lord, a young gentleman waits outside with letters from the doctor.
Bring him in and let us see the letters.

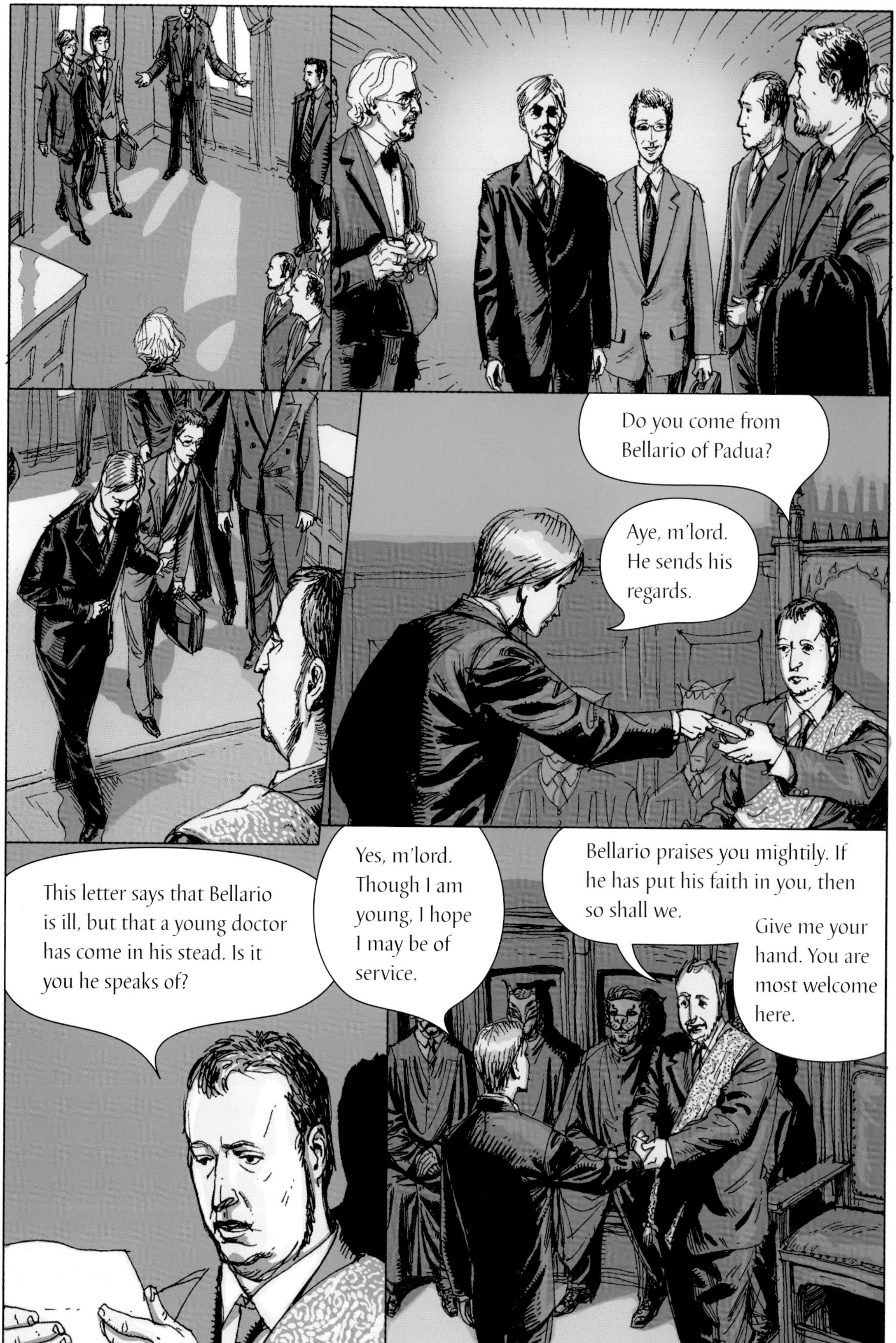
Do you come from Bellario of Padua?
Aye, m'lord. He sends his regards.
This letter says that Bellario is ill, but that a young doctor has come in his stead. Is it you he speaks of?
Yes, m'lord. Though I am young, I hope I may be of service.
Bellario praises you mightily. If he has put his faith in you, then so shall we.
Give me your hand. You are most welcome here.

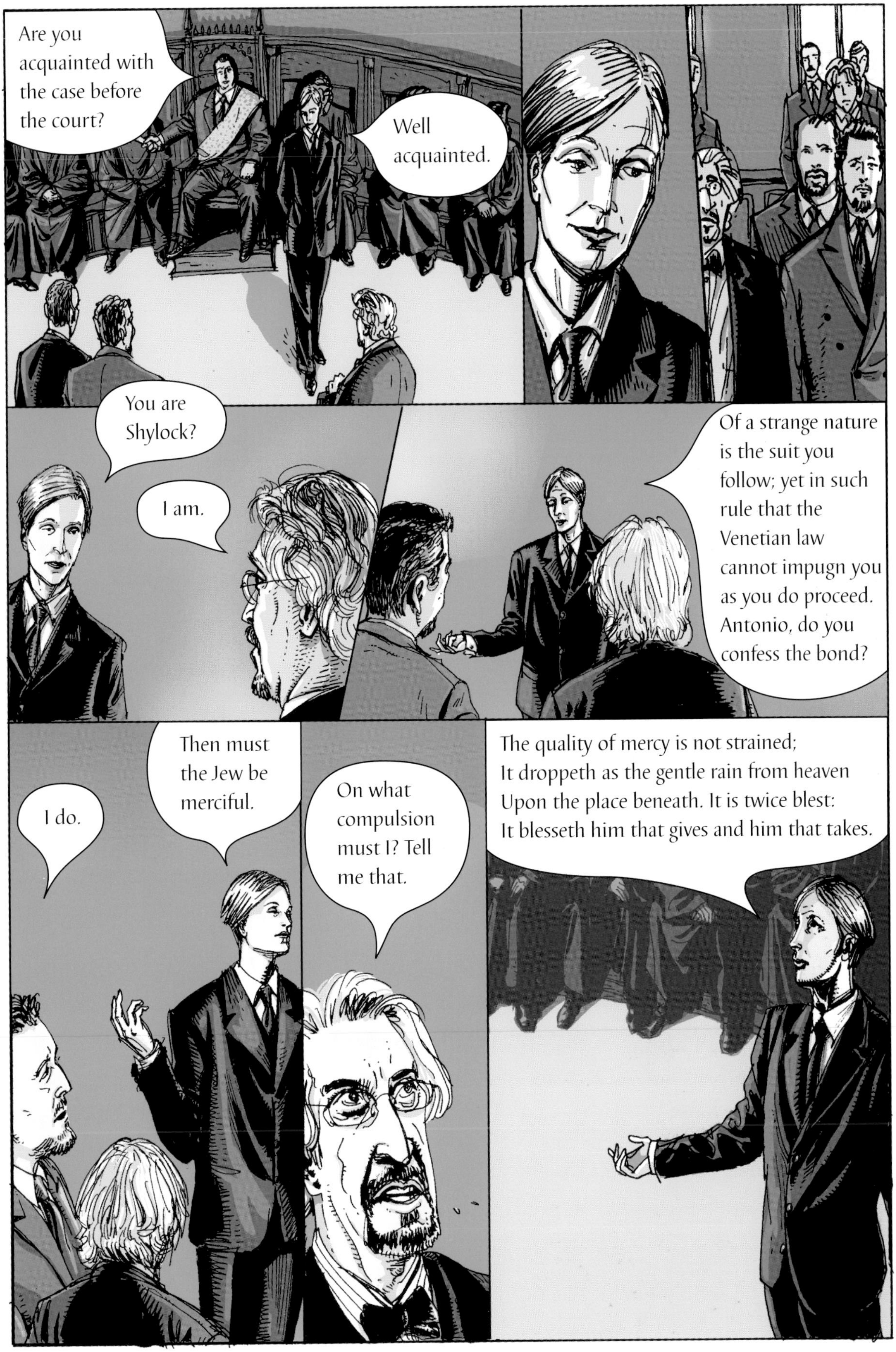
Are you acquainted with the case before the court?
Well acquainted.
You are Shylock?
I am.
Of a strange nature is the suit you follow; yet in such rule that the Venetian law cannot impugn you as you do proceed. Antonio, do you confess the bond?
I do.
Then must the Jew be merciful.
On what compulsion must I? Tell me that.
The quality of mercy is not strained;
It droppeth as the gentle rain from heaven
Upon the place beneath. It is twice blest:
It blesseth him that gives and him that takes.

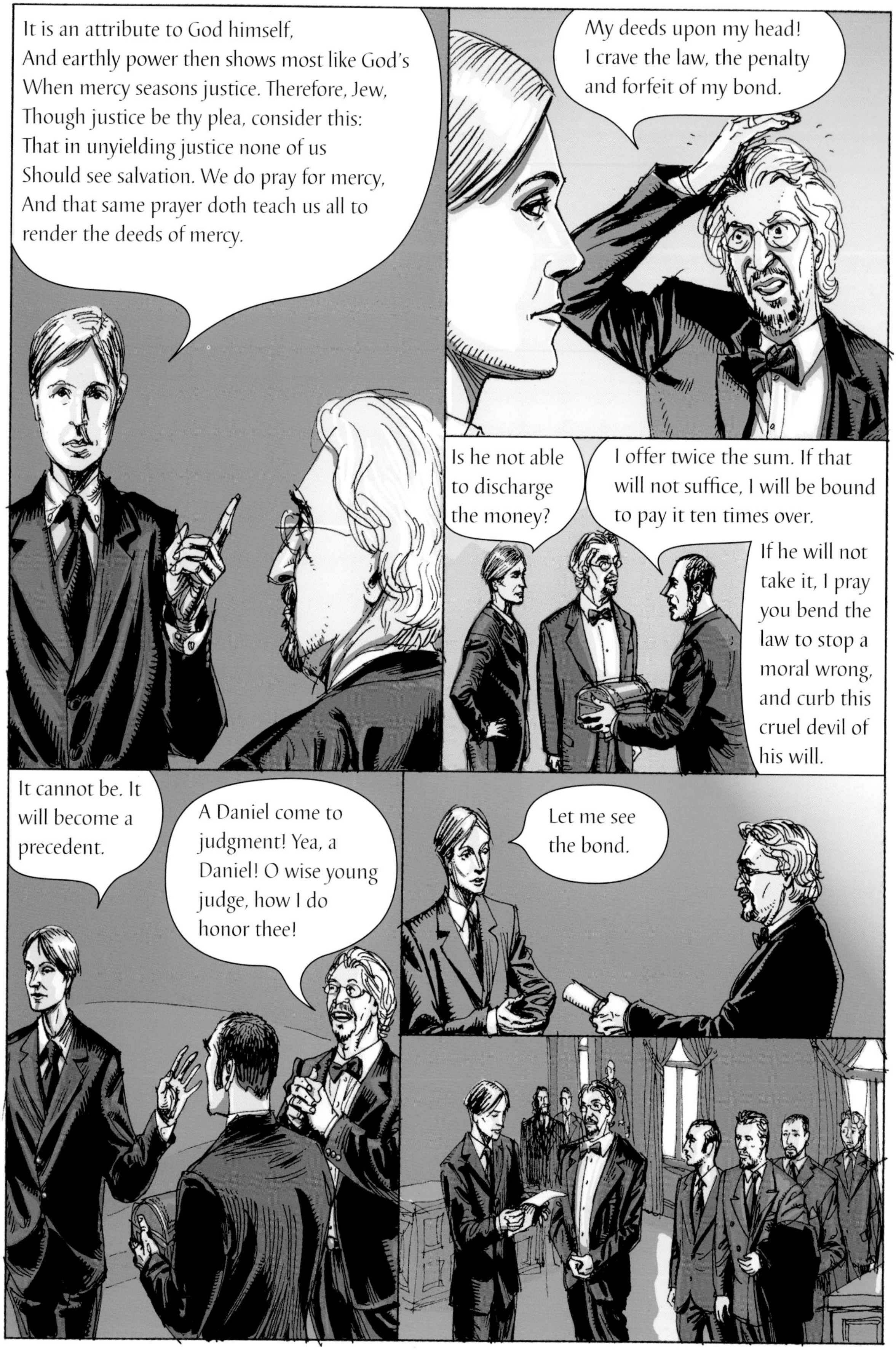
It is an attribute to God himself,
And earthly power then shows most like God's
When mercy seasons justice. Therefore, Jew,
Though justice be thy plea, consider this:
That in unyielding justice none of us
Should see salvation. We do pray for mercy,
And that same prayer doth teach us all to
render the deeds of mercy.
My deeds upon my head! I crave the law, the penalty and forfeit of my bond.
Is he not able to discharge the money?
I offer twice the sum. If that will not suffice, I will be bound to pay it ten times over.
If he will not take it, I pray you bend the law to stop a moral wrong, and curb this cruel devil of his will.
It cannot be. It will become a precedent.
A Daniel come to judgment! Yea, a Daniel! O wise young judge, how I do honor thee!
Let me see the bond.

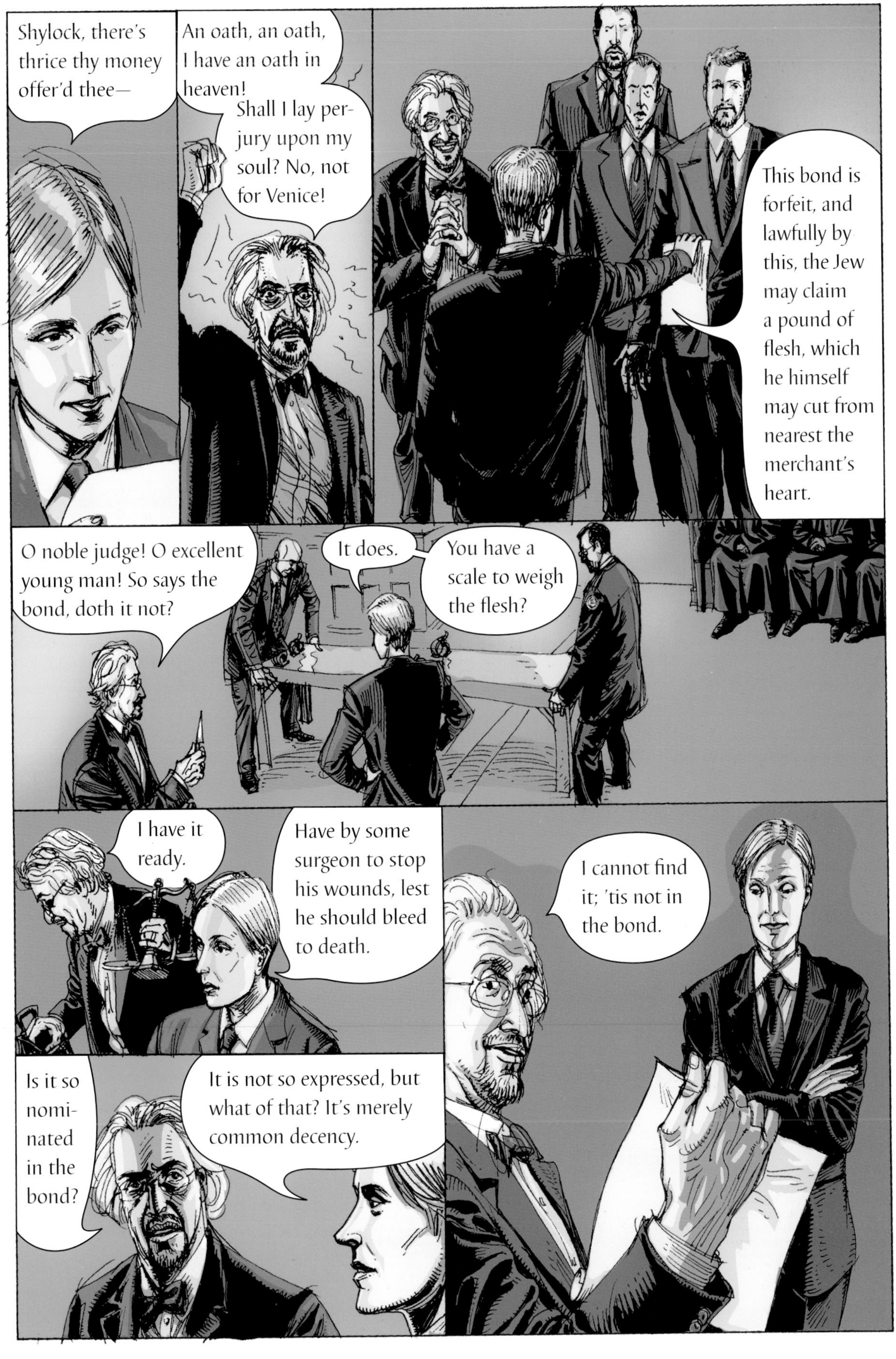
Shylock, there's thrice thy money offer'd thee—
An oath, an oath, I have an oath in heaven!
Shall I lay perjury upon my soul? No, not for Venice!
This bond is forfeit, and lawfully by this, the Jew may claim a pound of flesh, which he himself may cut from nearest the merchant's heart.
O noble judge! O excellent young man! So says the bond, doth it not?
It does.
You have a scale to weigh the flesh?
I have it ready.
Have by some surgeon to stop his wounds, lest he should bleed to death.
Is it so nominated in the bond?
It is not so expressed, but what of that? It's merely common decency.
I cannot find it; 'tis not in the bond.

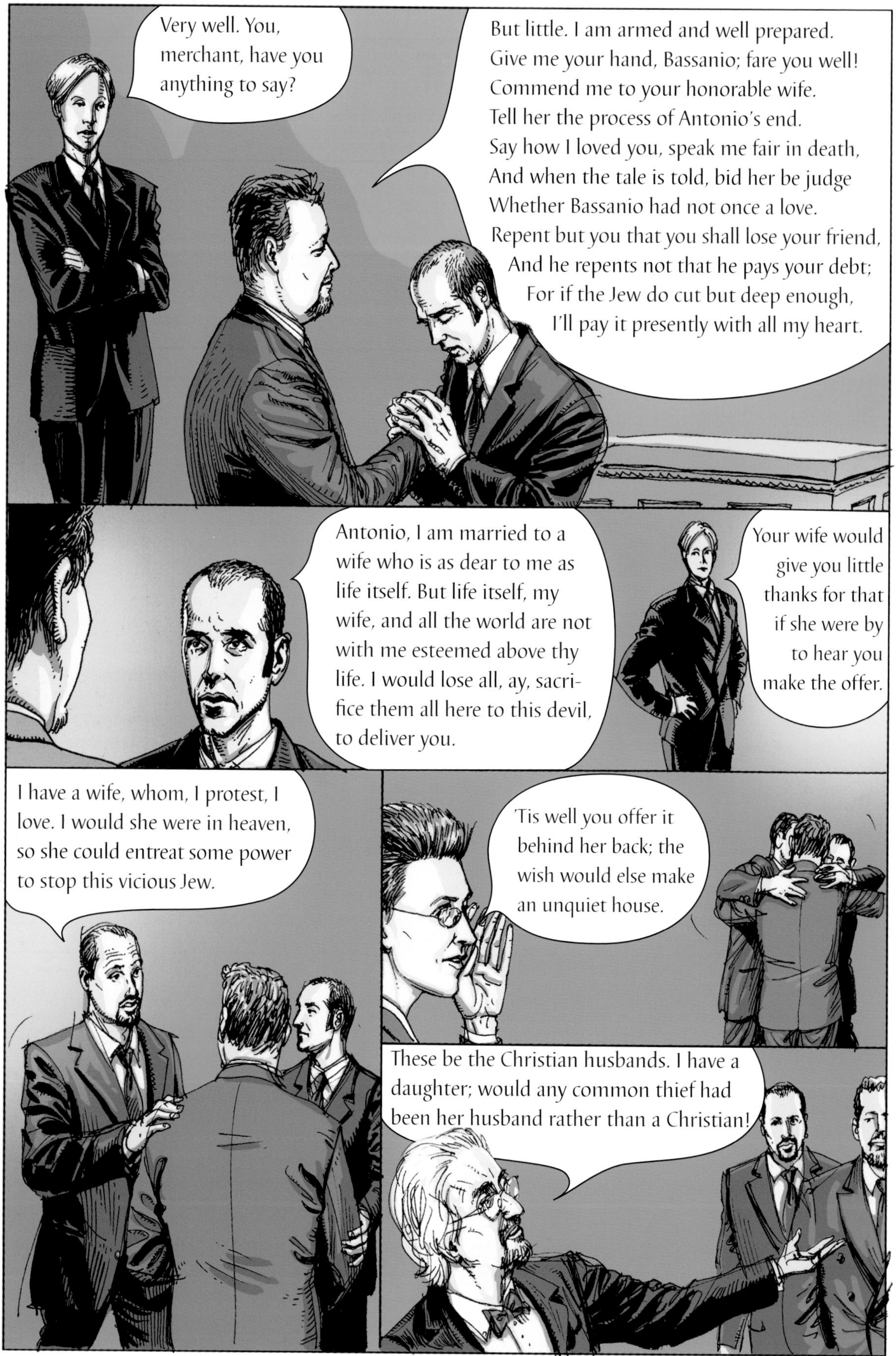

Very well. You, merchant, have you anything to say?
But little. I am armed and well prepared. Give me your hand, Bassanio; fare you well! Commend me to your honorable wife. Tell her the process of Antonio's end. Say how I loved you, speak me fair in death, And when the tale is told, bid her be judge Whether Bassanio had not once a love. Repent but you that you shall lose your friend, And he repents not that he pays your debt; For if the Jew do cut but deep enough, I'll pay it presently with all my heart.
Antonio, I am married to a wife who is as dear to me as life itself. But life itself, my wife, and all the world are not with me esteemed above thy life. I would lose all, ay, sacrifice them all here to this devil, to deliver you.
Your wife would give you little thanks for that if she were by to hear you make the offer.
I have a wife, whom, I protest, I love. I would she were in heaven, so she could entreat some power to stop this vicious Jew.
'Tis well you offer it behind her back; the wish would else make an unquiet house.
These be the Christian husbands. I have a daughter; would any common thief had been her husband rather than a Christian!

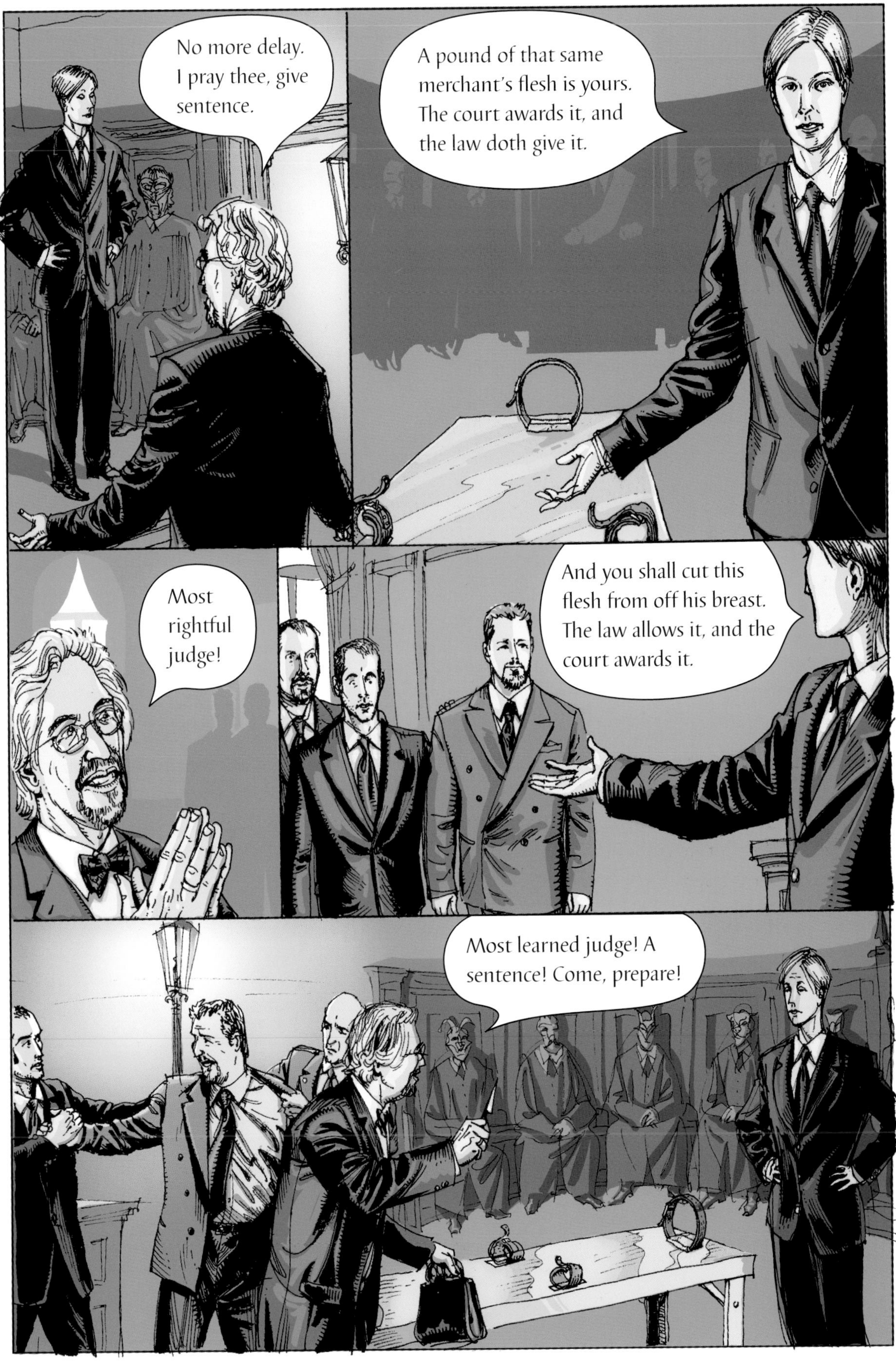
No more delay. I pray thee, give sentence.
A pound of that same merchant's flesh is yours. The court awards it, and the law doth give it.
Most rightful judge!
And you shall cut this flesh from off his breast. The law allows it, and the court awards it.
Most learned judge! A sentence! Come, prepare!

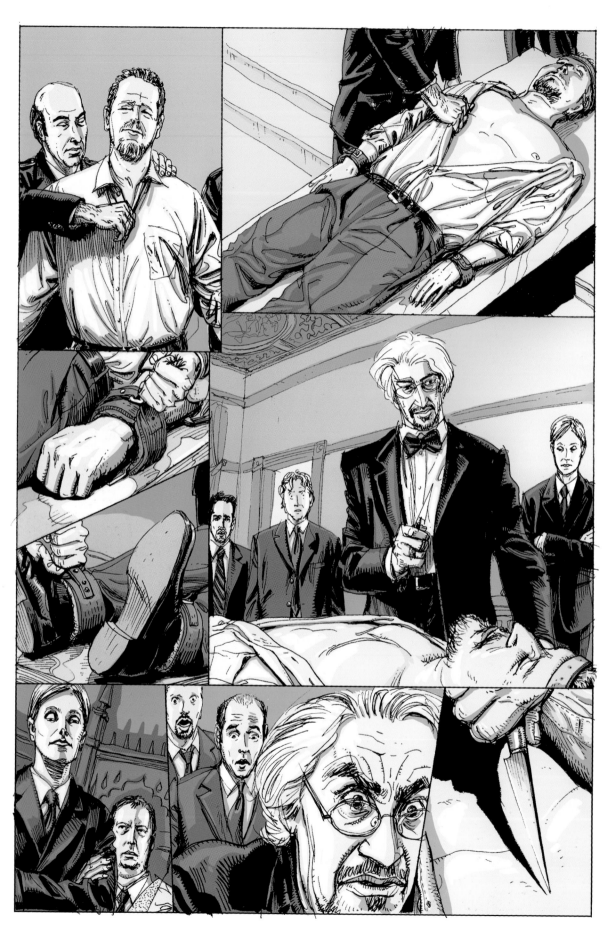

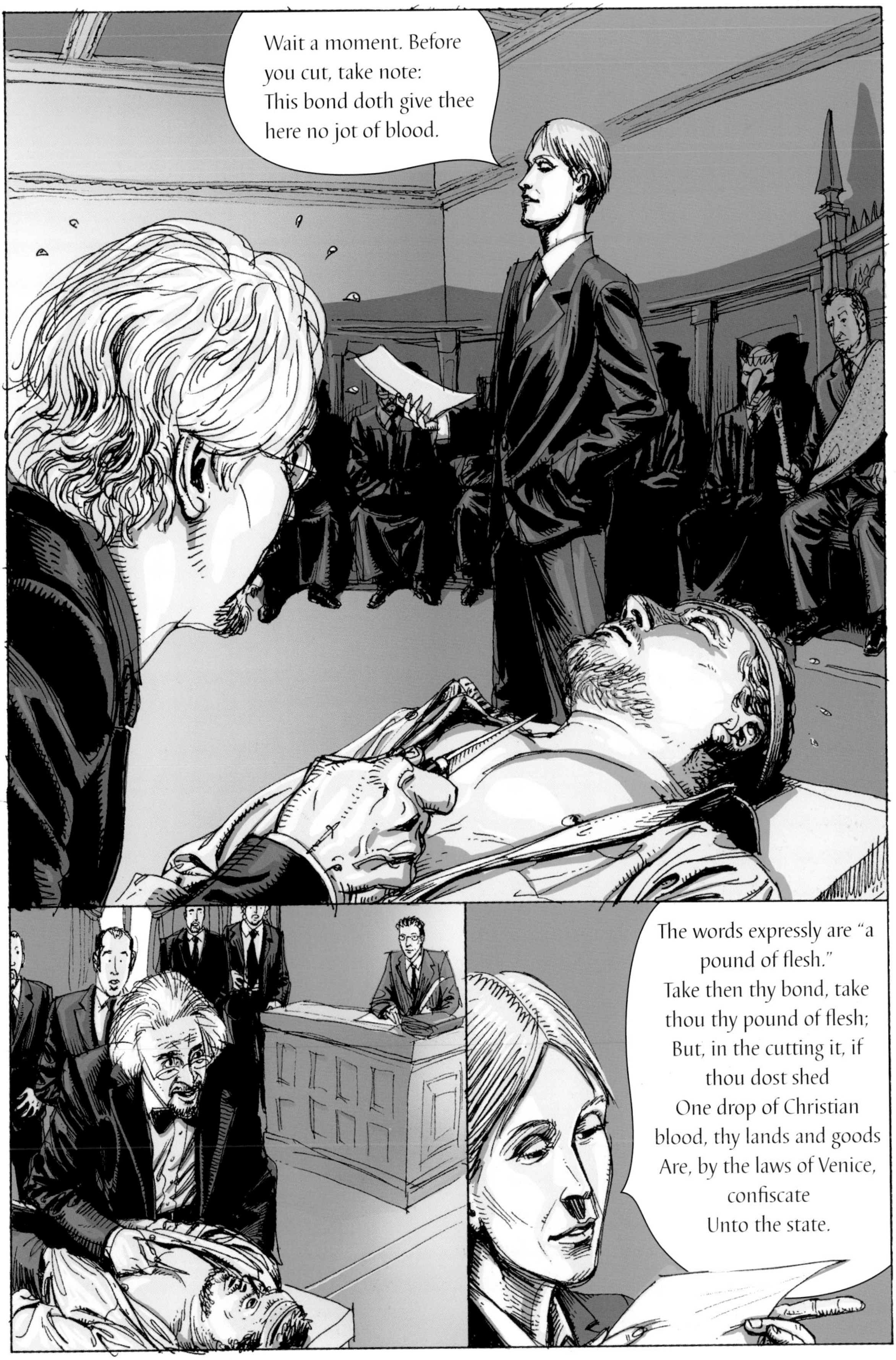
Wait a moment. Before you cut, take note: This bond doth give thee here no jot of blood.
The words expressly are "a pound of flesh." Take then thy bond, take thou thy pound of flesh; But, in the cutting it, if thou dost shed One drop of Christian blood, thy lands and goods Are, by the laws of Venice, confiscate Unto the state.

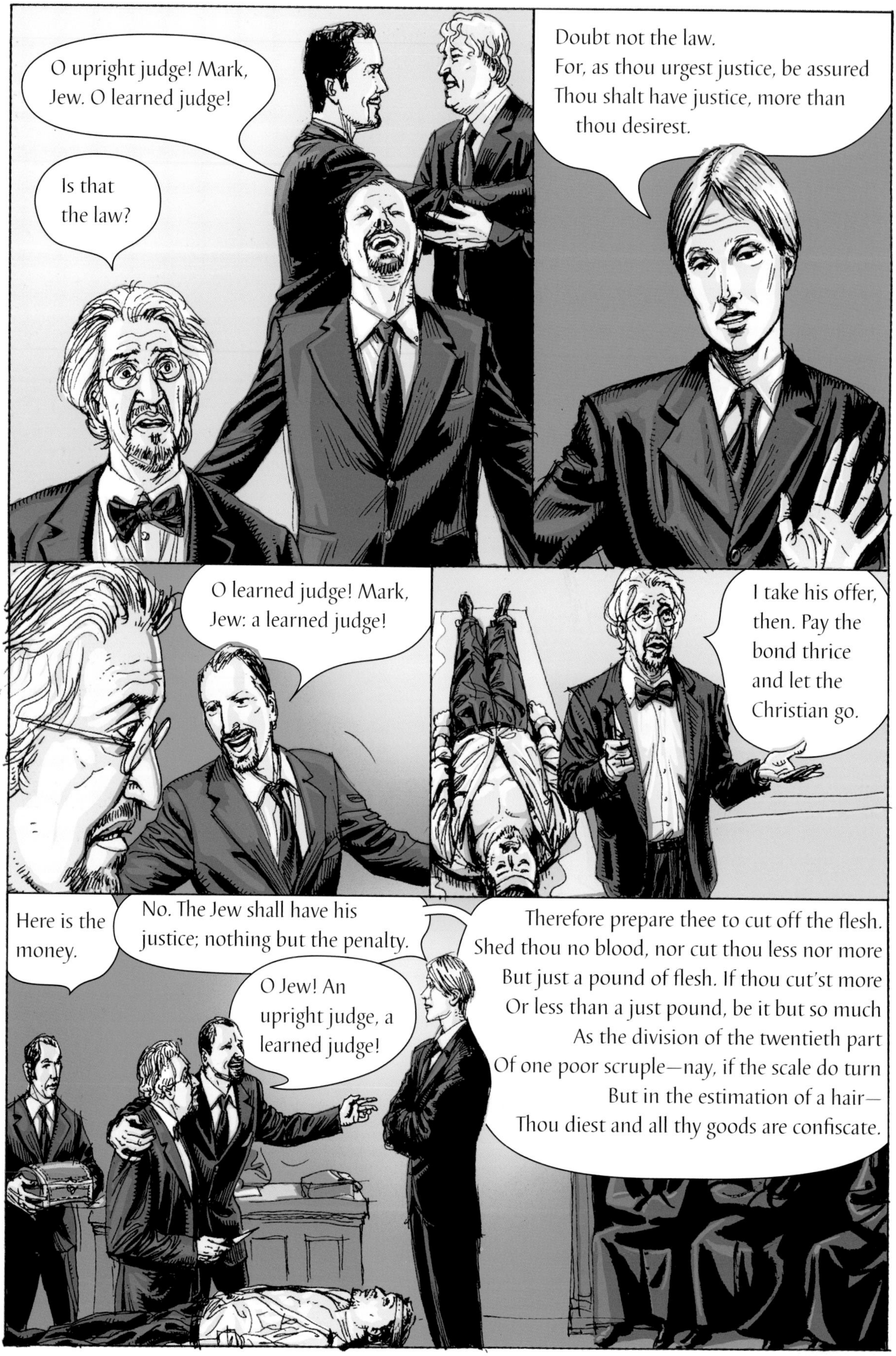
O upright judge! Mark, Jew. O learned judge!
Is that the law?
Doubt not the law. For, as thou urgest justice, be assured Thou shalt have justice, more than thou desirest.
O learned judge! Mark, Jew: a learned judge!
I take his offer, then. Pay the bond thrice and let the Christian go.
Here is the money.
No. The Jew shall have his justice; nothing but the penalty.
O Jew! An upright judge, a learned judge!
Therefore prepare thee to cut off the flesh. Shed thou no blood, nor cut thou less nor more But just a pound of flesh. If thou cut'st more Or less than a just pound, be it but so much As the division of the twentieth part Of one poor scruple—nay, if the scale do turn But in the estimation of a hair— Thou diest and all thy goods are confiscate.

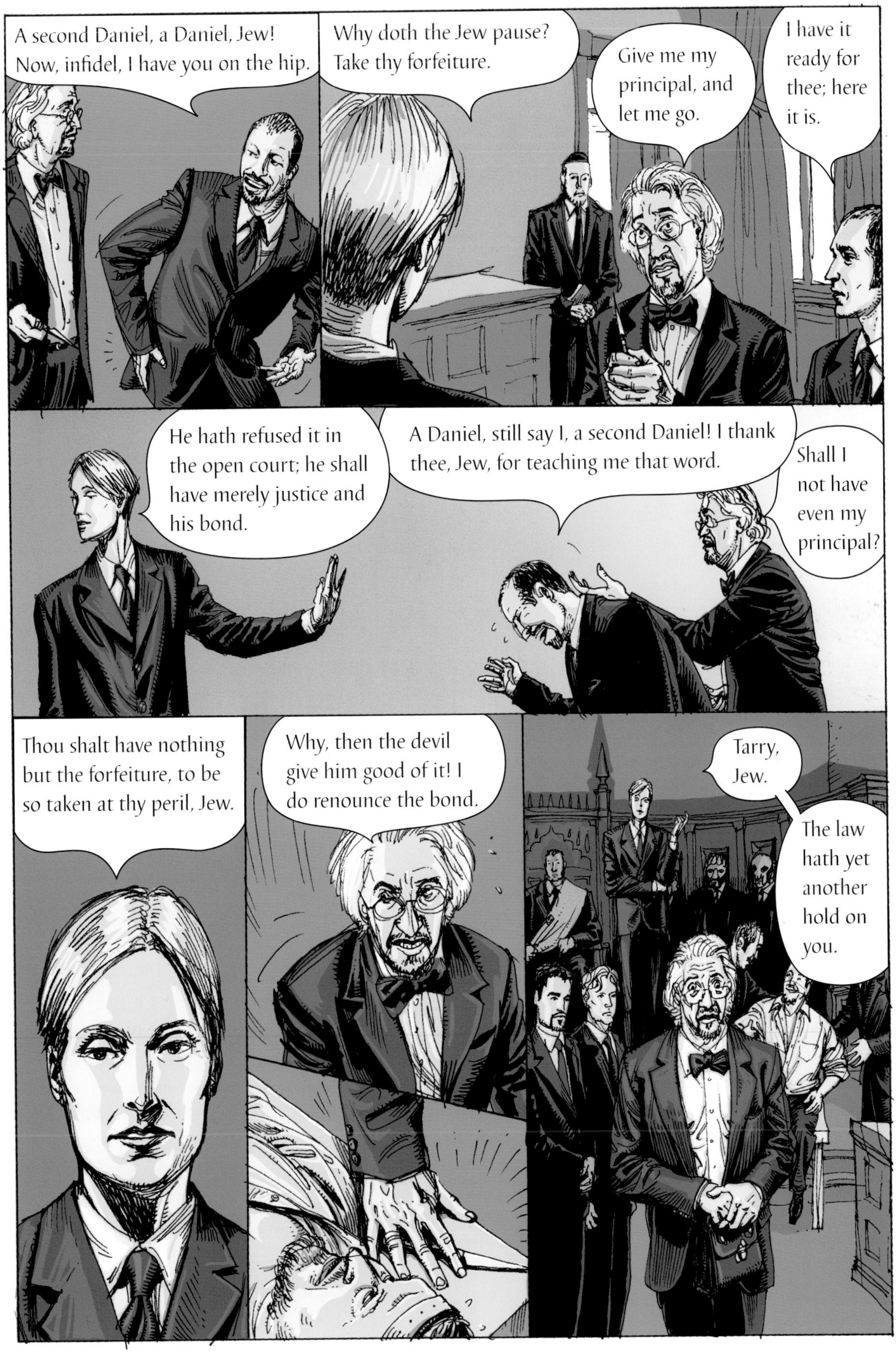
A second Daniel, a Daniel, Jew! Now, infidel, I have you on the hip.
Why doth the Jew pause? Take thy forfeiture.
Give me my principal, and let me go.
I have it ready for thee; here it is.
He hath refused it in the open court; he shall have merely justice and his bond.
A Daniel, still say I, a second Daniel! I thank thee, Jew, for teaching me that word.
Shall I not have even my principal?
Thou shalt have nothing but the forfeiture, to be so taken at thy peril, Jew.
Why, then the devil give him good of it! I do renounce the bond.
Tarry, Jew.
The law hath yet another hold on you.

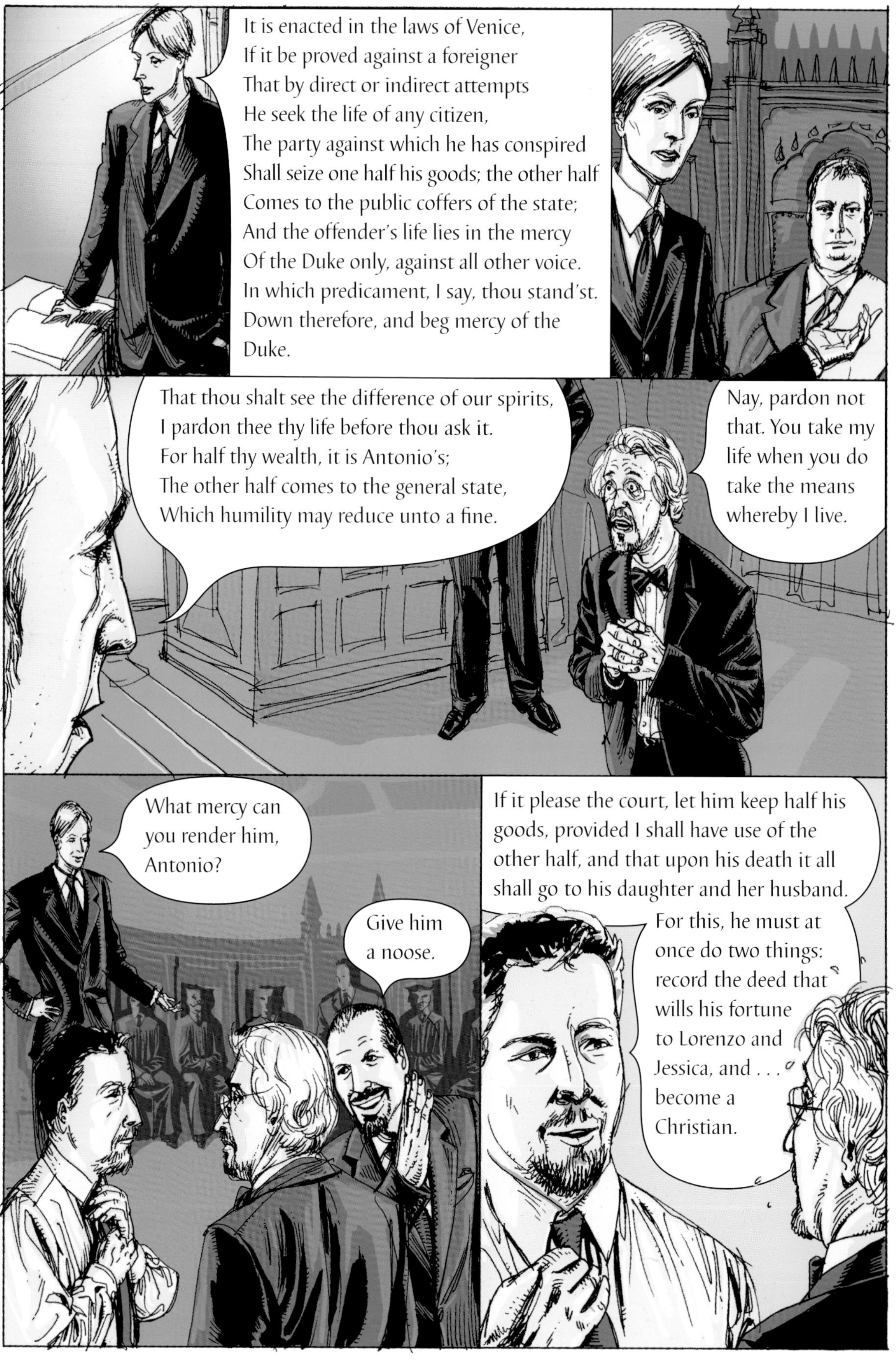
It is enacted in the laws of Venice,
If it be proved against a foreigner
That by direct or indirect attempts
He seek the life of any citizen,
The party against which he has conspired
Shall seize one half his goods; the other half
Comes to the public coffers of the state;
And the offender's life lies in the mercy
Of the Duke only, against all other voice.
In which predicament, I say, thou stand'st.
Down therefore, and beg mercy of the Duke.
That thou shalt see the difference of our spirits,
I pardon thee thy life before thou ask it.
For half thy wealth, it is Antonio's;
The other half comes to the general state,
Which humility may reduce unto a fine.
Nay, pardon not that. You take my life when you do take the means whereby I live.
What mercy can you render him, Antonio?
Give him a noose.
If it please the court, let him keep half his goods, provided I shall have use of the other half, and that upon his death it all shall go to his daughter and her husband.
For this, he must at once do two things: record the deed that wills his fortune to Lorenzo and Jessica, and . . . become a Christian.

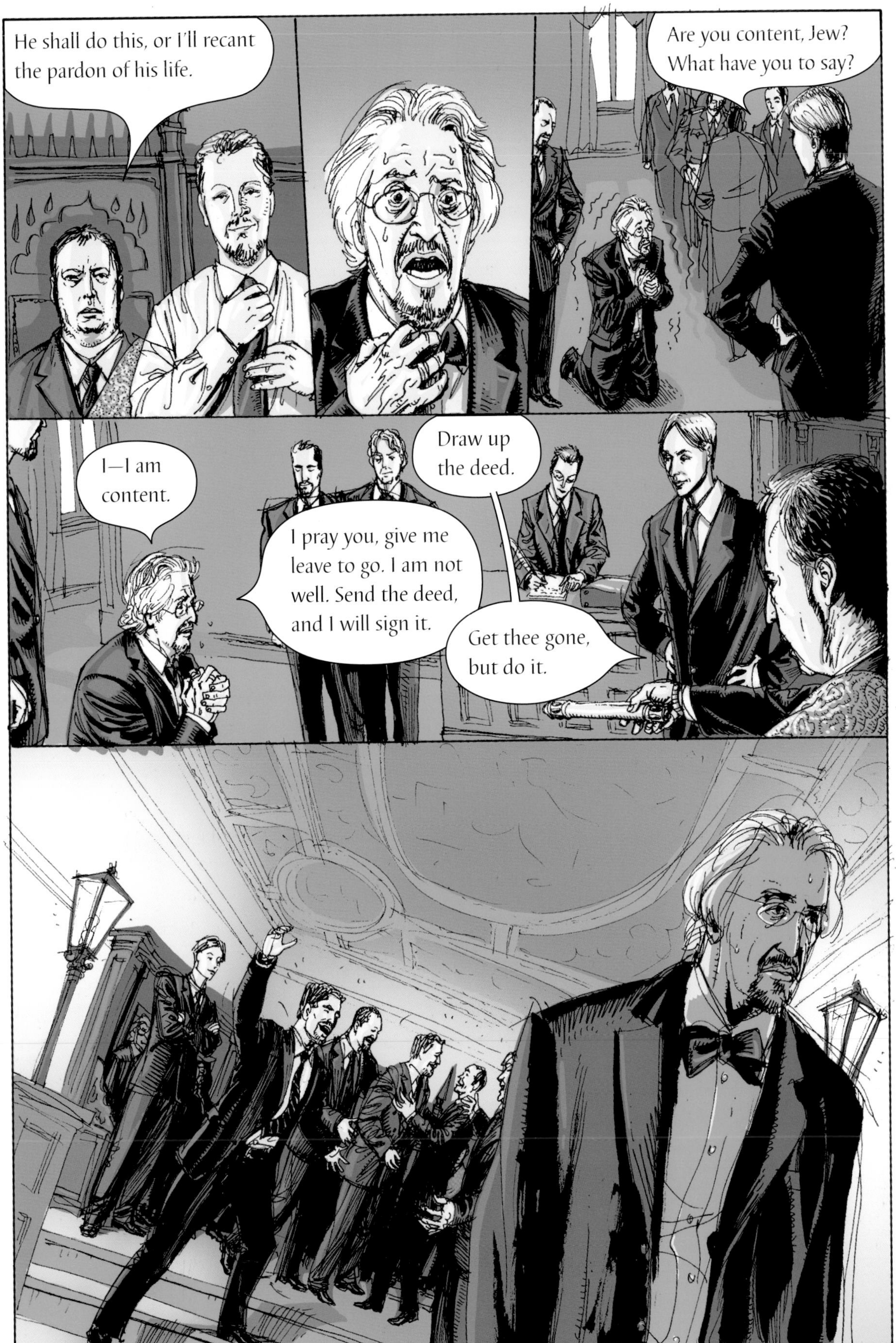
He shall do this, or I'll recant the pardon of his life.
Are you content, Jew? What have you to say?
I—I am content.
I pray you, give me leave to go. I am not well. Send the deed, and I will sign it.
Draw up the deed.
Get thee gone, but do it.

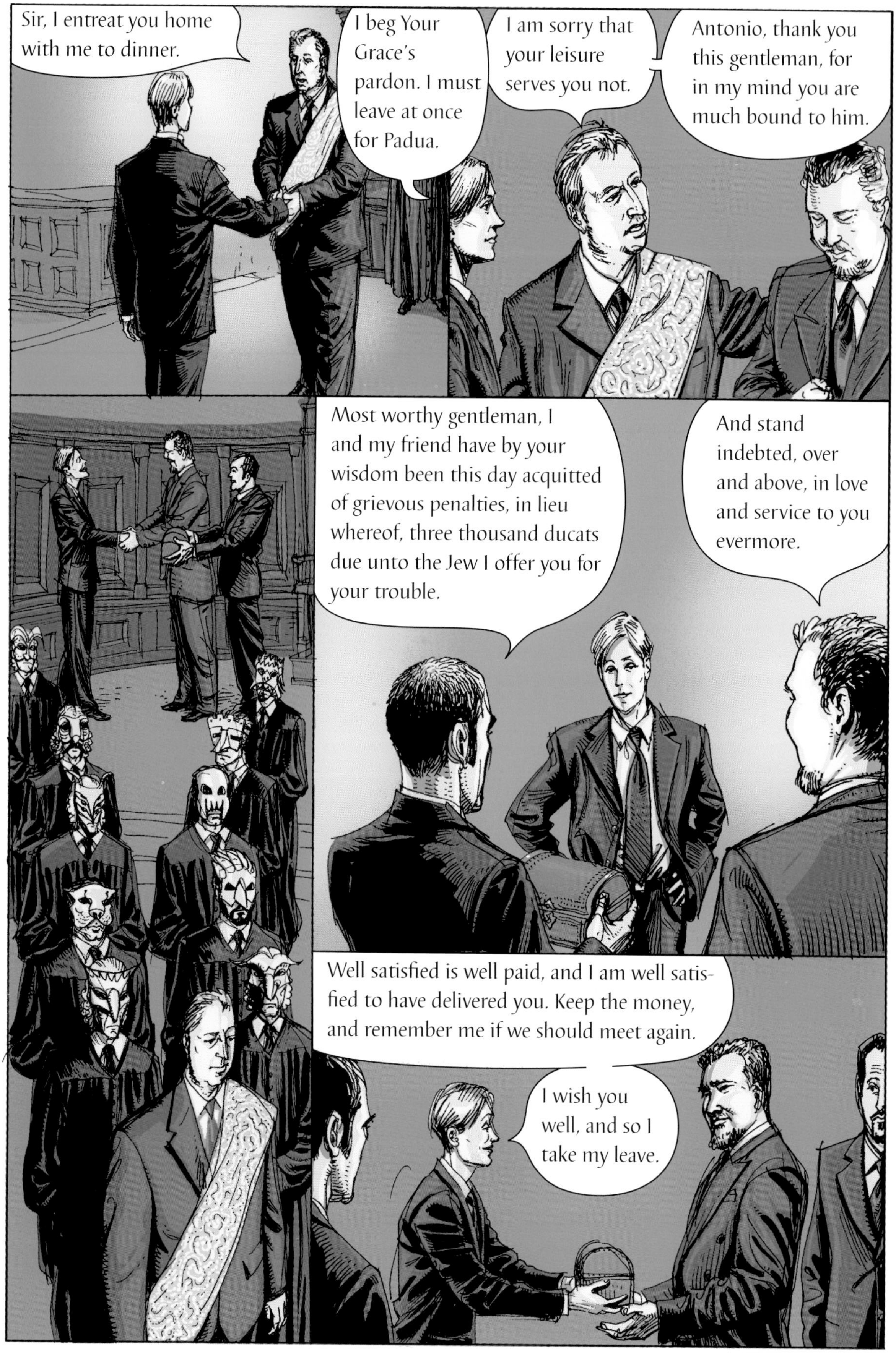
Sir, I entreat you home with me to dinner.
I beg Your Grace's pardon. I must leave at once for Padua.
I am sorry that your leisure serves you not.
Antonio, thank you this gentleman, for in my mind you are much bound to him.
Most worthy gentleman, I and my friend have by your wisdom been this day acquitted of grievous penalties, in lieu whereof, three thousand ducats due unto the Jew I offer you for your trouble.
And stand indebted, over and above, in love and service to you evermore.
Well satisfied is well paid, and I am well satisfied to have delivered you. Keep the money, and remember me if we should meet again.
I wish you well, and so I take my leave.

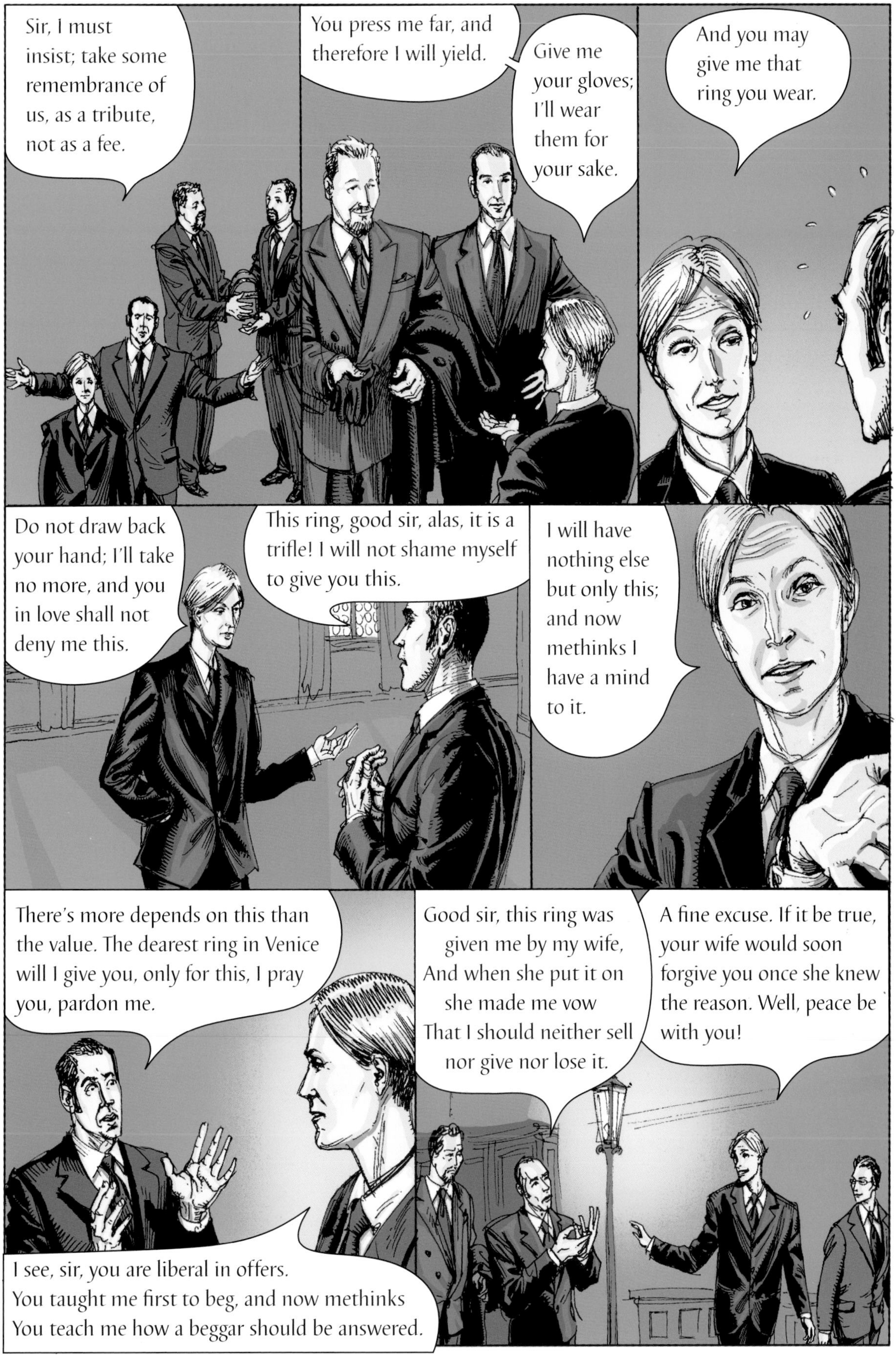

Sir, I must insist; take some remembrance of us, as a tribute, not as a fee.
You press me far, and therefore I will yield.
Give me your gloves; I'll wear them for your sake.
And you may give me that ring you wear.
Do not draw back your hand; I'll take no more, and you in love shall not deny me this.
This ring, good sir, alas, it is a trifle! I will not shame myself to give you this.
I will have nothing else but only this; and now methinks I have a mind to it.
There's more depends on this than the value. The dearest ring in Venice will I give you, only for this, I pray you, pardon me.
I see, sir, you are liberal in offers.
You taught me first to beg, and now methinks
You teach me how a beggar should be answered.
Good sir, this ring was given me by my wife,
And when she put it on she made me vow
That I should neither sell nor give nor lose it.
A fine excuse. If it be true, your wife would soon forgive you once she knew the reason. Well, peace be with you!

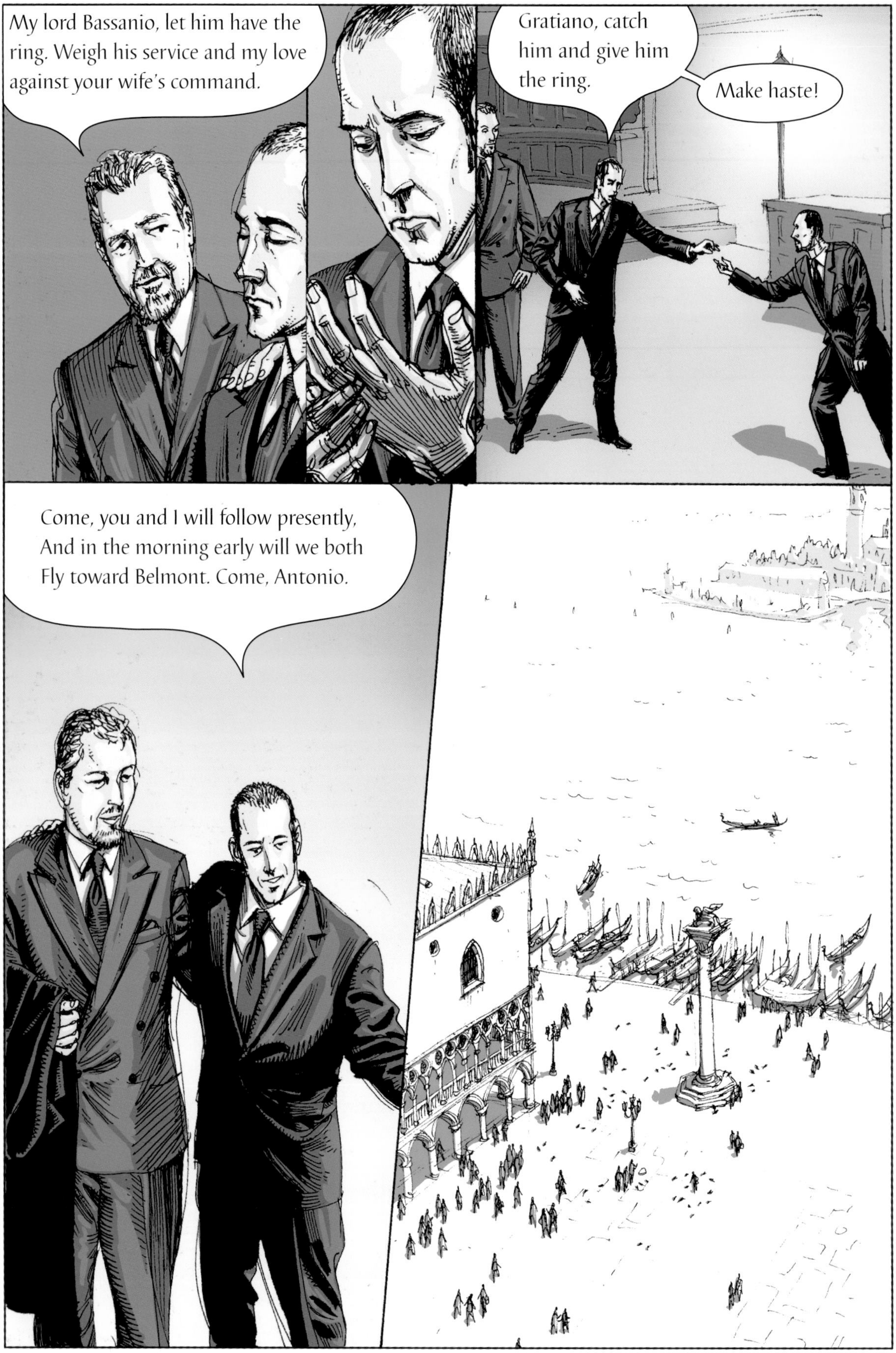
My lord Bassanio, let him have the ring. Weigh his service and my love against your wife's command.
Gratiano, catch him and give him the ring.
Make haste!
Come, you and I will follow presently, And in the morning early will we both Fly toward Belmont. Come, Antonio.

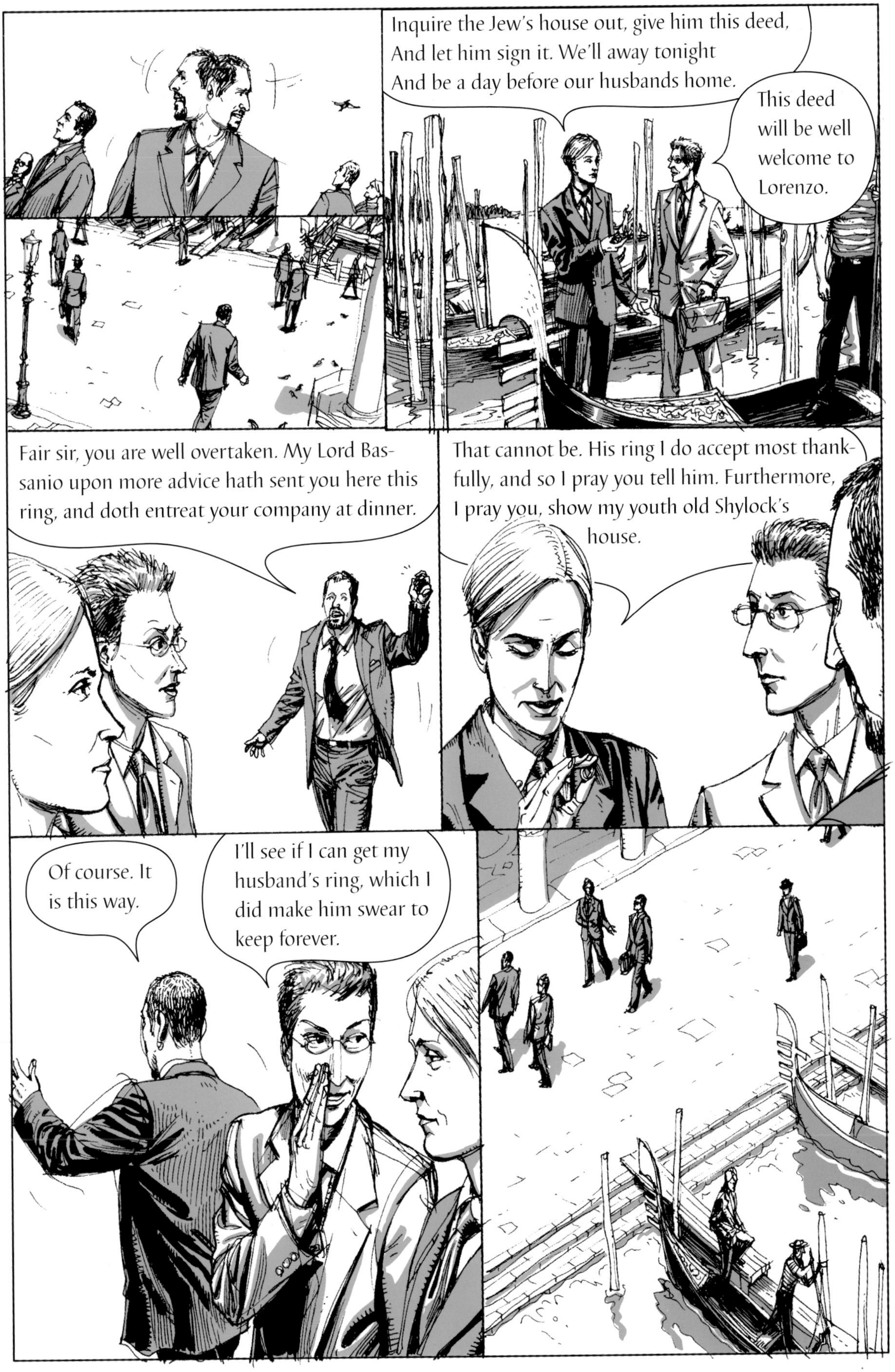
Inquire the Jew's house out, give him this deed, And let him sign it. We'll away tonight And be a day before our husbands home.
This deed will be well welcome to Lorenzo.
Fair sir, you are well overtaken. My Lord Bassanio upon more advice hath sent you here this ring, and doth entreat your company at dinner.
That cannot be. His ring I do accept most thankfully, and so I pray you tell him. Furthermore, I pray you, show my youth old Shylock's house.
Of course. It is this way.
I'll see if I can get my husband's ring, which I did make him swear to keep forever.

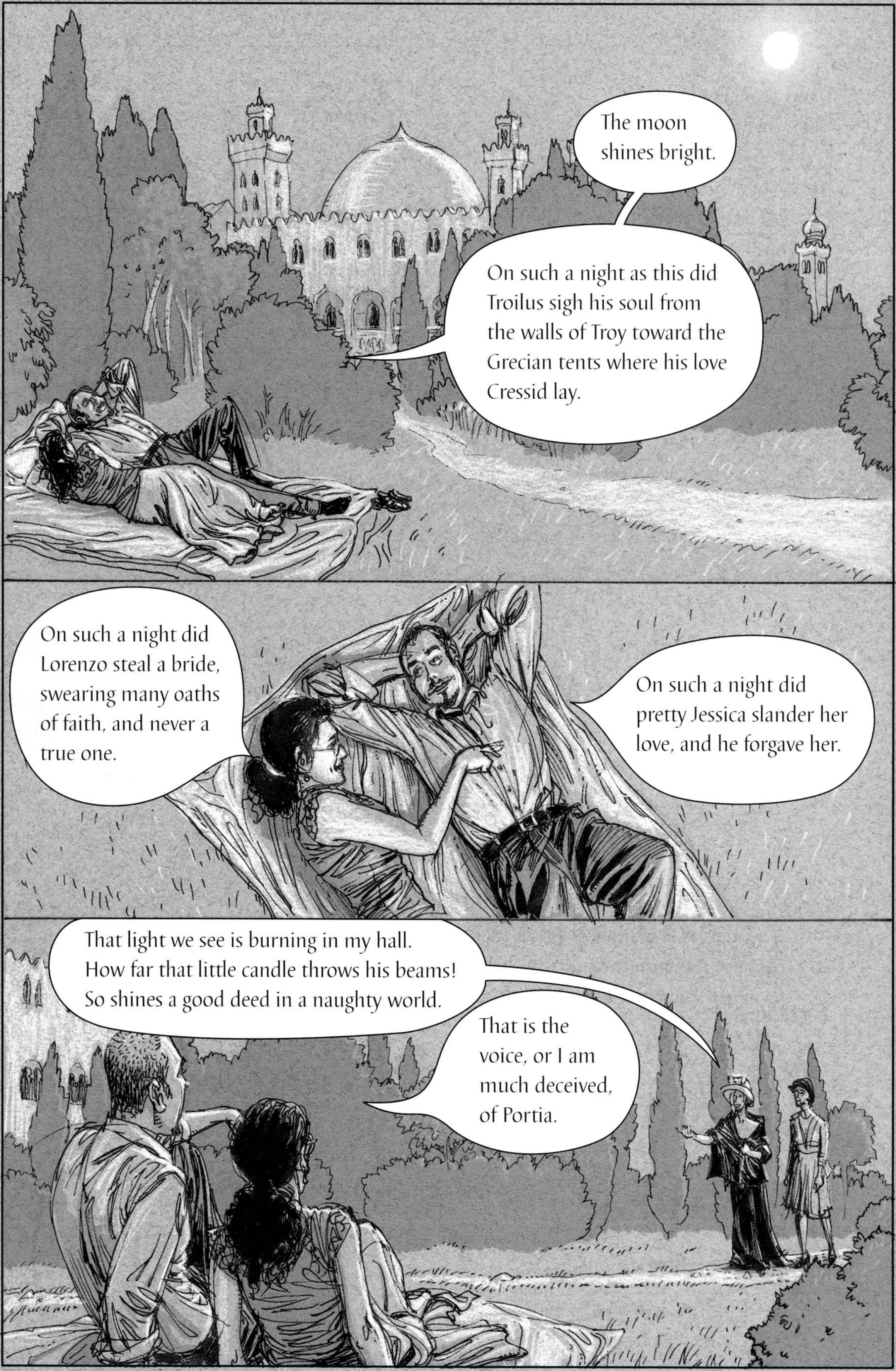
The moon shines bright.
On such a night as this did Troilus sigh his soul from the walls of Troy toward the Grecian tents where his love Cressid lay.
On such a night did Lorenzo steal a bride, swearing many oaths of faith, and never a true one.
On such a night did pretty Jessica slander her love, and he forgave her.
That light we see is burning in my hall. How far that little candle throws his beams! So shines a good deed in a naughty world.
That is the voice, or I am much deceived, of Portia.

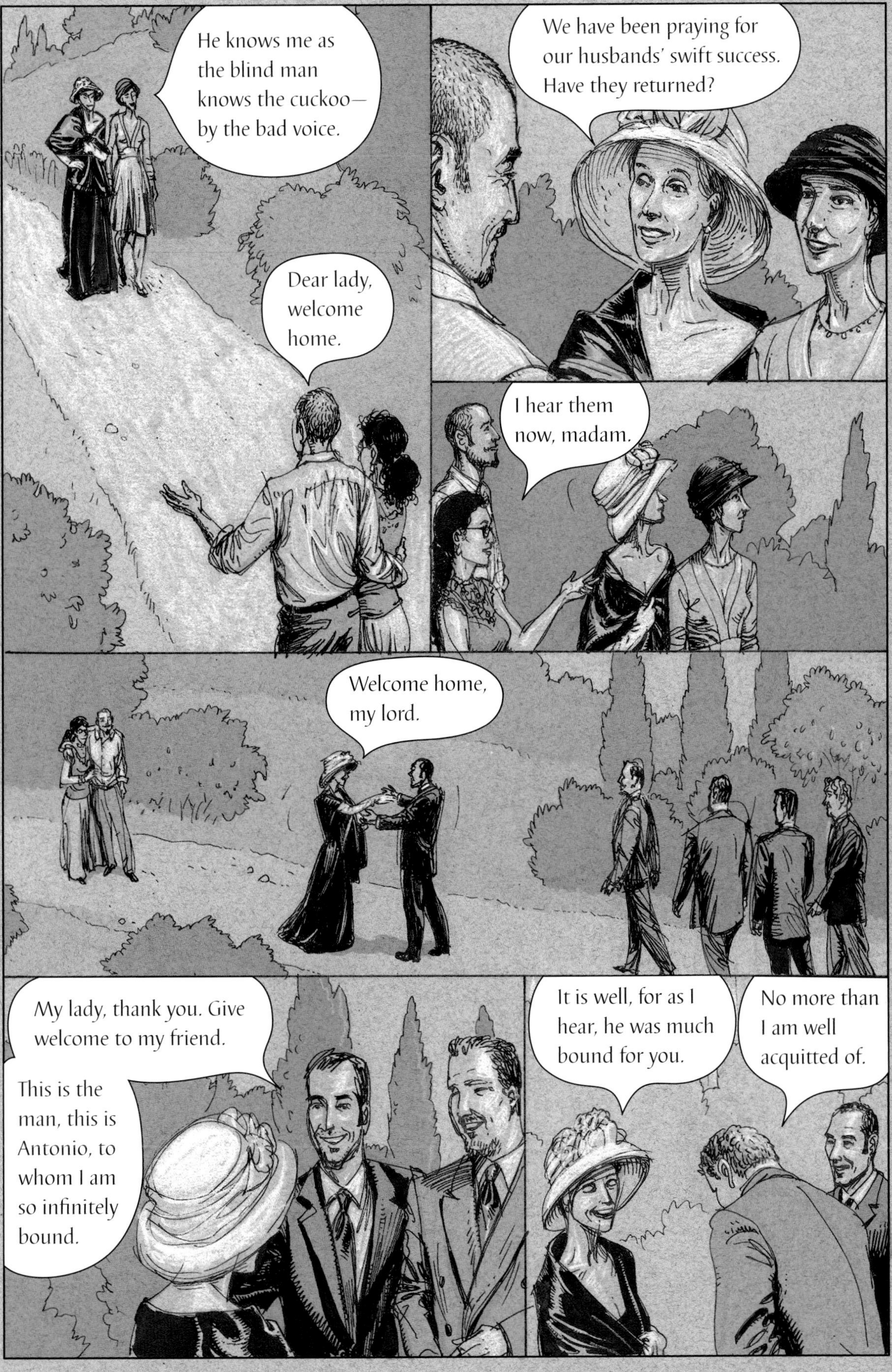
He knows me as the blind man knows the cuckoo— by the bad voice.
We have been praying for our husbands' swift success. Have they returned?
Dear lady, welcome home.
I hear them now, madam.
Welcome home, my lord.
My lady, thank you. Give welcome to my friend.
This is the man, this is Antonio, to whom I am so infinitely bound.
It is well, for as I hear, he was much bound for you.
No more than I am well acquitted of.

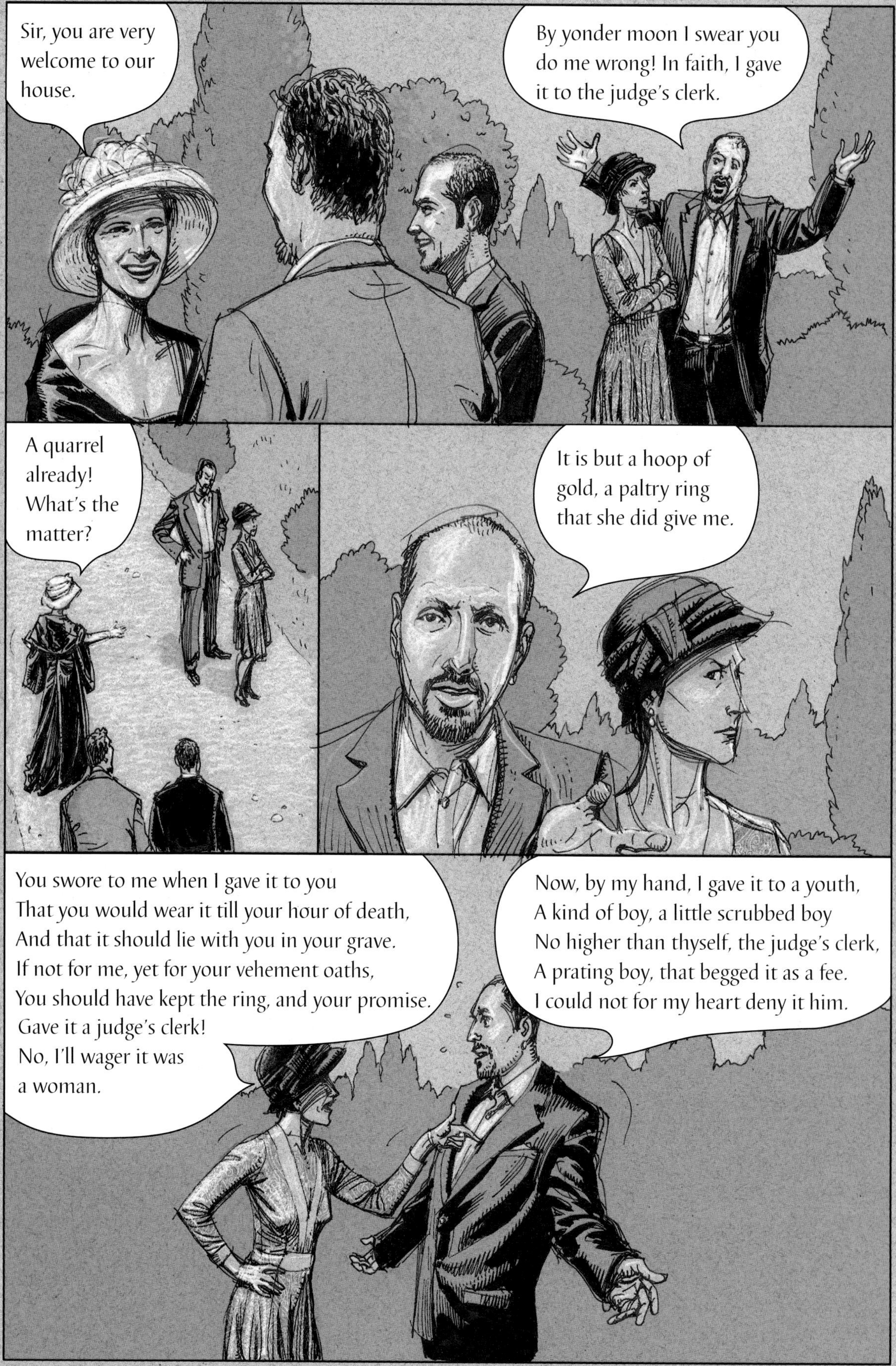

Sir, you are very welcome to our house.
By yonder moon I swear you do me wrong! In faith, I gave it to the judge's clerk.
A quarrel already! What's the matter?
It is but a hoop of gold, a paltry ring that she did give me.
You swore to me when I gave it to you
That you would wear it till your hour of death,
And that it should lie with you in your grave.
If not for me, yet for your vehement oaths,
You should have kept the ring, and your promise.
Gave it a judge's clerk!
No, I'll wager it was a woman.
Now, by my hand, I gave it to a youth,
A kind of boy, a little scrubbed boy
No higher than thyself, the judge's clerk,
A prating boy, that begged it as a fee.
I could not for my heart deny it him.

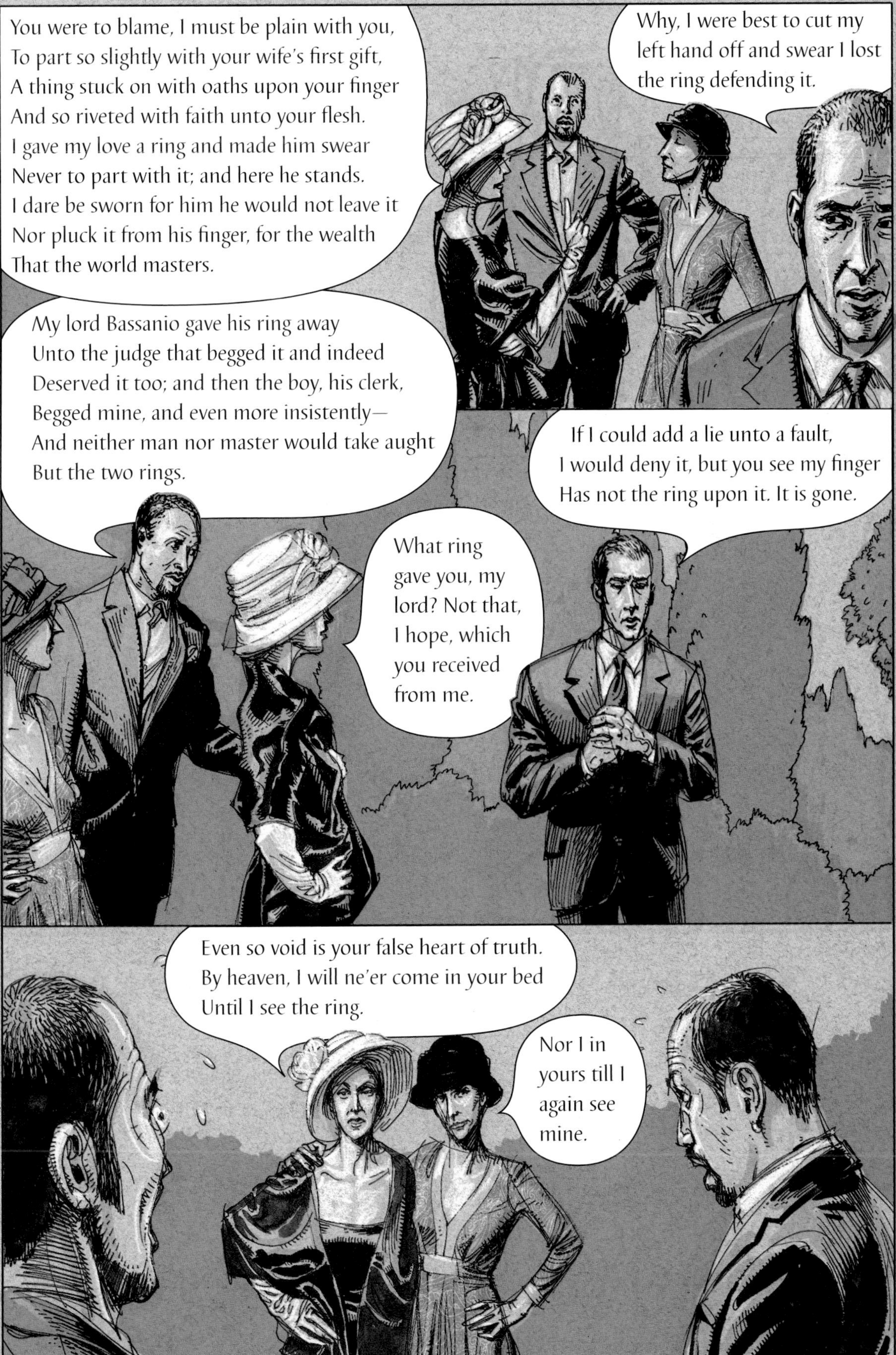
You were to blame, I must be plain with you, To part so slightly with your wife's first gift, A thing stuck on with oaths upon your finger And so riveted with faith unto your flesh. I gave my love a ring and made him swear Never to part with it; and here he stands. I dare be sworn for him he would not leave it Nor pluck it from his finger, for the wealth That the world masters.
Why, I were best to cut my left hand off and swear I lost the ring defending it.
My lord Bassanio gave his ring away Unto the judge that begged it and indeed Deserved it too; and then the boy, his clerk, Begged mine, and even more insistently— And neither man nor master would take aught But the two rings.
What ring gave you, my lord? Not that, I hope, which you received from me.
If I could add a lie unto a fault, I would deny it, but you see my finger Has not the ring upon it. It is gone.
Even so void is your false heart of truth. By heaven, I will ne'er come in your bed Until I see the ring.
Nor I in yours till I again see mine.

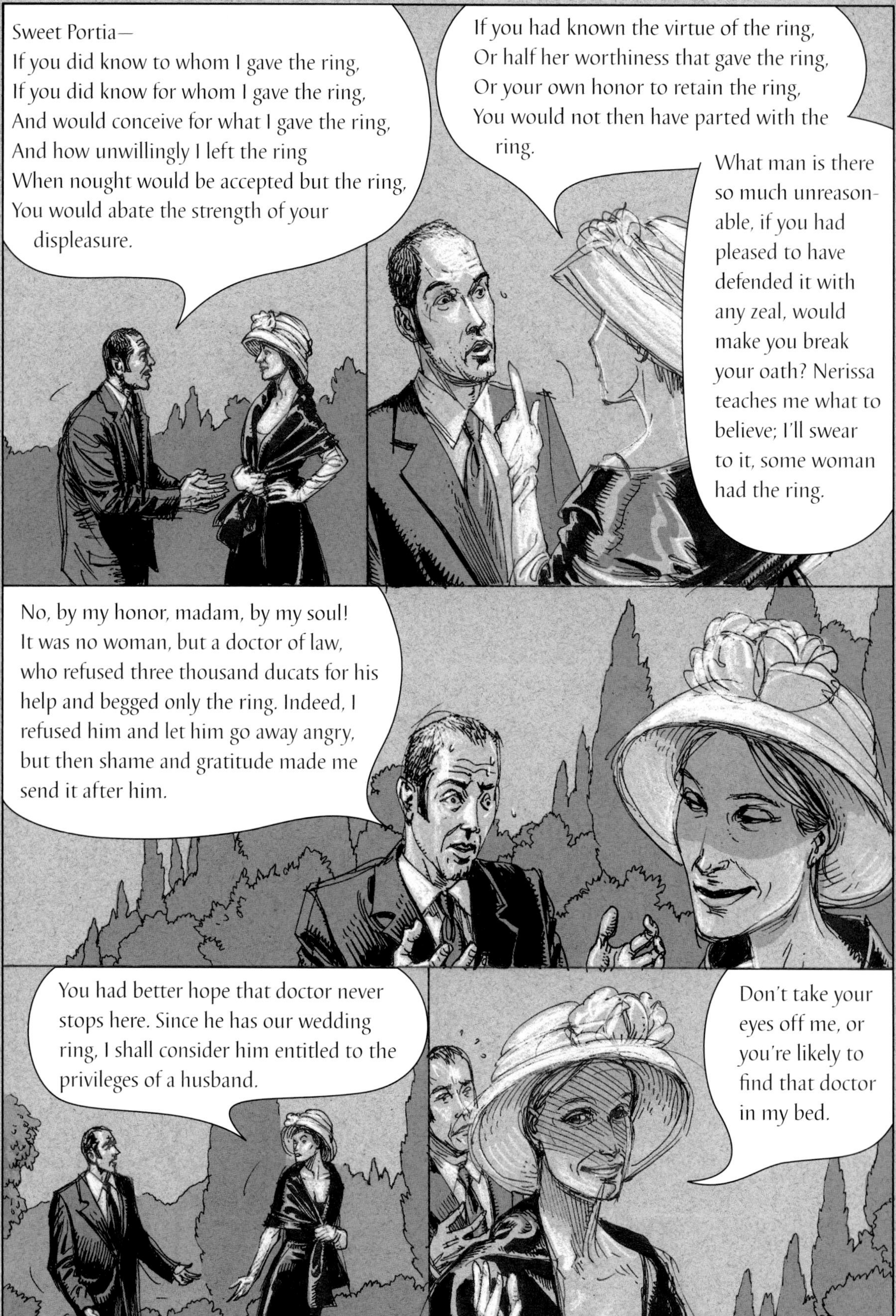
Sweet Portia— If you did know to whom I gave the ring, If you did know for whom I gave the ring, And would conceive for what I gave the ring, And how unwillingly I left the ring When nought would be accepted but the ring, You would abate the strength of your displeasure.
If you had known the virtue of the ring, Or half her worthiness that gave the ring, Or your own honor to retain the ring, You would not then have parted with the ring.
What man is there so much unreasonable, if you had pleased to have defended it with any zeal, would make you break your oath? Nerissa teaches me what to believe; I'll swear to it, some woman had the ring.
No, by my honor, madam, by my soul! It was no woman, but a doctor of law, who refused three thousand ducats for his help and begged only the ring. Indeed, I refused him and let him go away angry, but then shame and gratitude made me send it after him.
You had better hope that doctor never stops here. Since he has our wedding ring, I shall consider him entitled to the privileges of a husband.
Don't take your eyes off me, or you're likely to find that doctor in my bed.

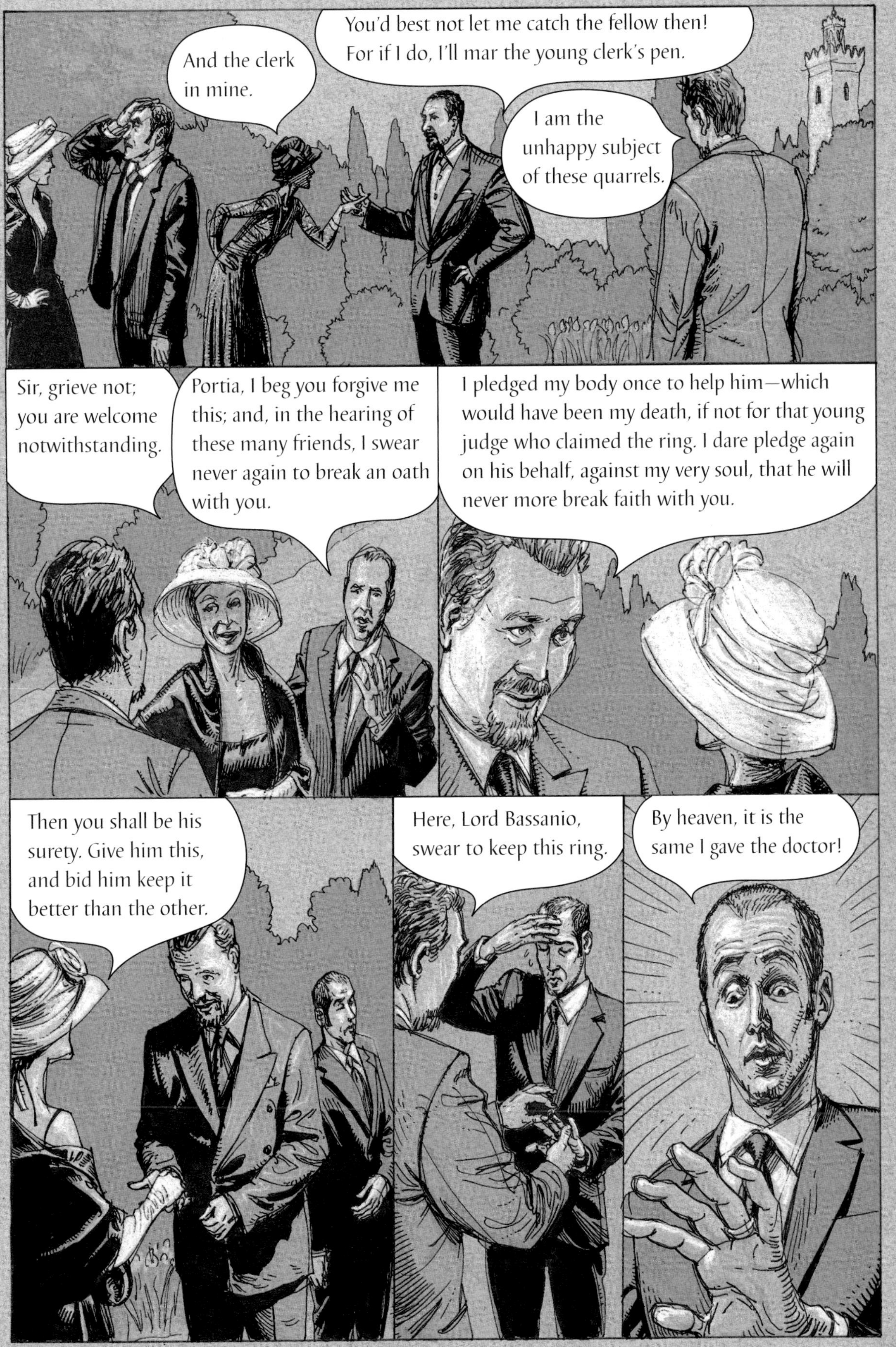
And the clerk in mine.
You'd best not let me catch the fellow then! For if I do, I'll mar the young clerk's pen.
I am the unhappy subject of these quarrels.
Sir, grieve not; you are welcome notwithstanding.
Portia, I beg you forgive me this; and, in the hearing of these many friends, I swear never again to break an oath with you.
I pledged my body once to help him—which would have been my death, if not for that young judge who claimed the ring. I dare pledge again on his behalf, against my very soul, that he will never more break faith with you.
Then you shall be his surety. Give him this, and bid him keep it better than the other.
Here, Lord Bassanio, swear to keep this ring.
By heaven, it is the same I gave the doctor!

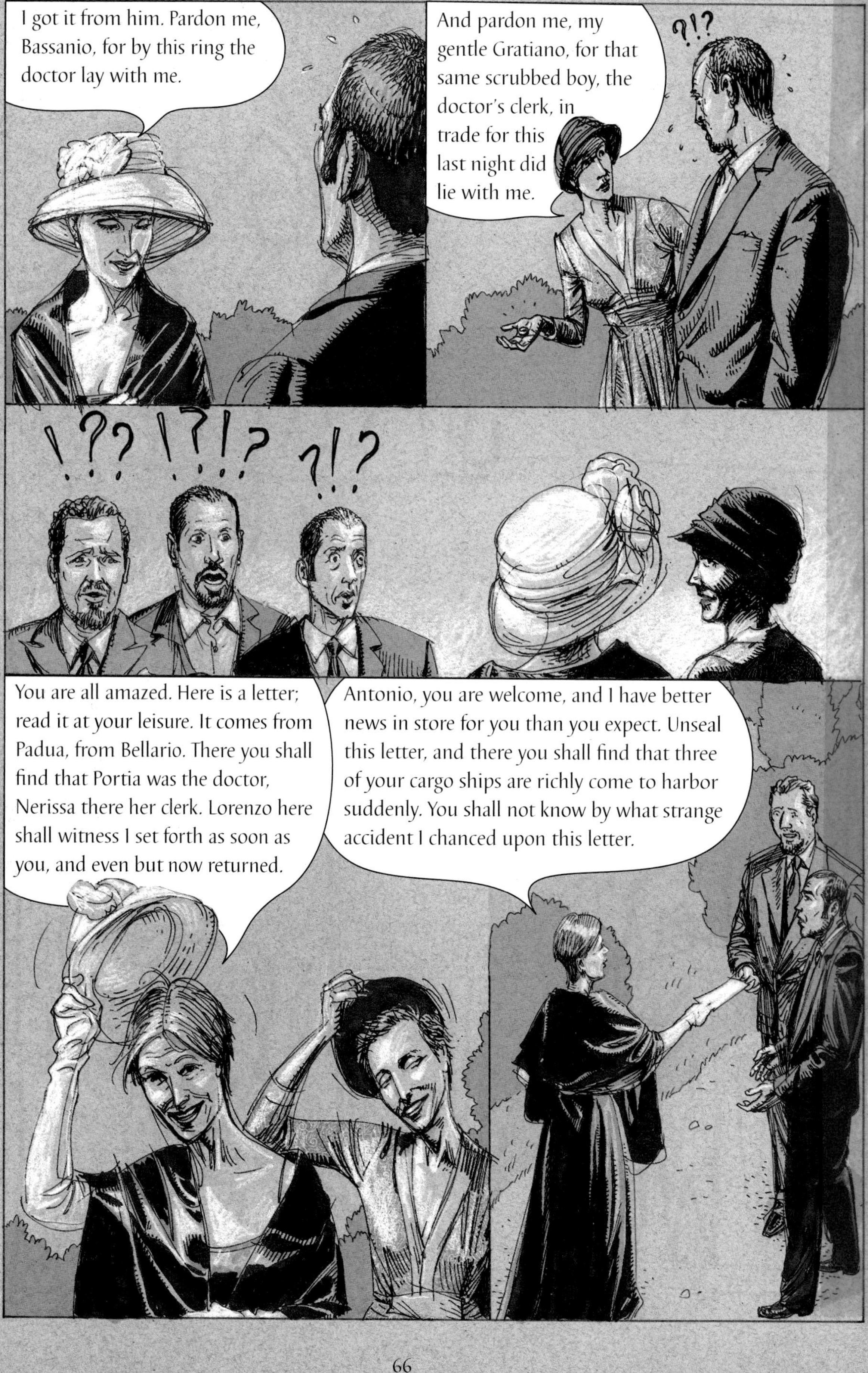
I got it from him. Pardon me, Bassanio, for by this ring the doctor lay with me.
And pardon me, my gentle Gratiano, for that same scrubbed boy, the doctor's clerk, in trade for this last night did lie with me.
?!?
!??
!?!?
?!?
You are all amazed. Here is a letter; read it at your leisure. It comes from Padua, from Bellario. There you shall find that Portia was the doctor, Nerissa there her clerk. Lorenzo here shall witness I set forth as soon as you, and even but now returned.
Antonio, you are welcome, and I have better news in store for you than you expect. Unseal this letter, and there you shall find that three of your cargo ships are richly come to harbor suddenly. You shall not know by what strange accident I chanced upon this letter.

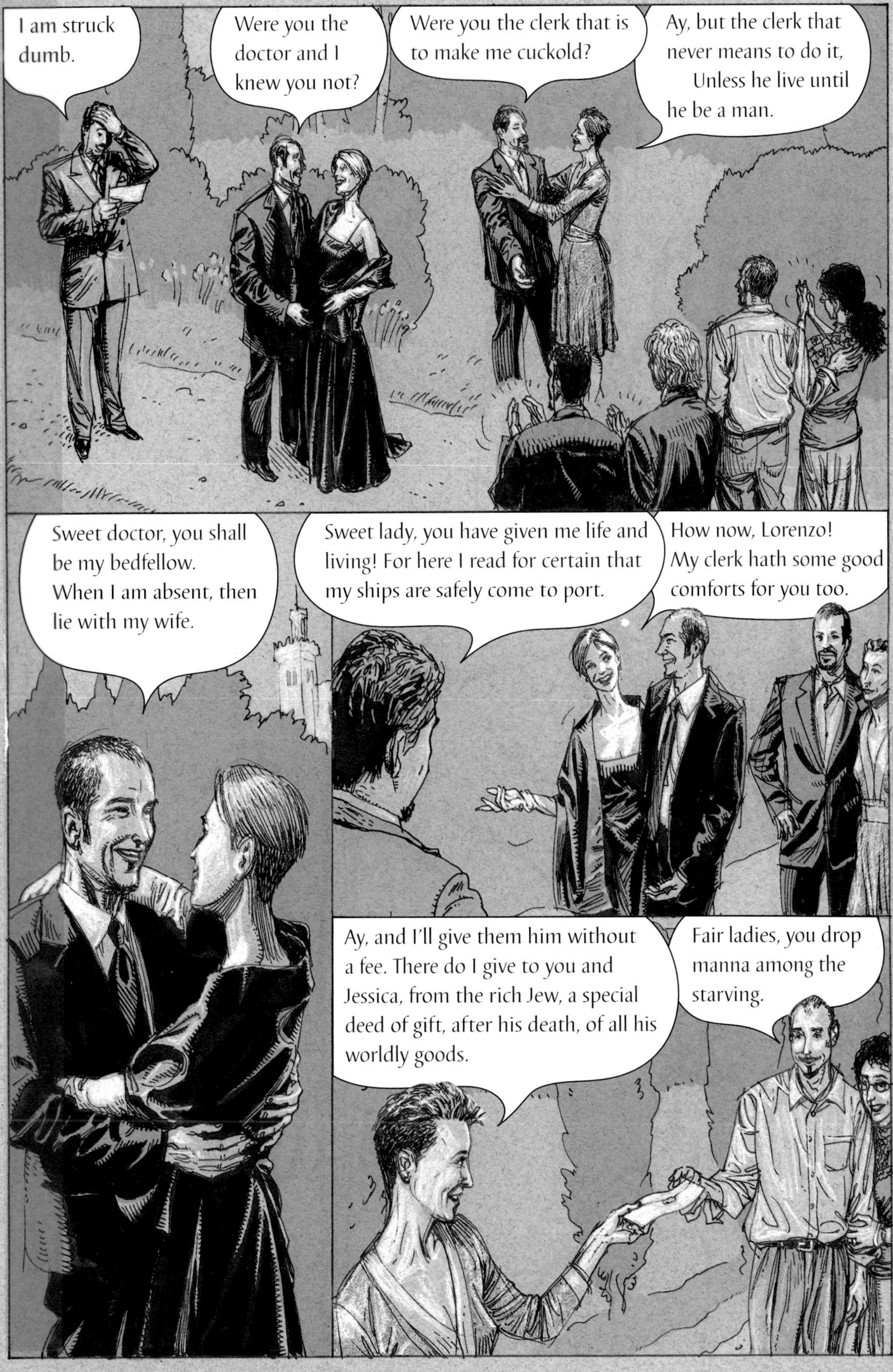
I am struck dumb.
Were you the doctor and I knew you not?
Were you the clerk that is to make me cuckold?
Ay, but the clerk that never means to do it, Unless he live until he be a man.
Sweet doctor, you shall be my bedfellow. When I am absent, then lie with my wife.
Sweet lady, you have given me life and living! For here I read for certain that my ships are safely come to port.
How now, Lorenzo! My clerk hath some good comforts for you too.
Ay, and I'll give them him without a fee. There do I give to you and Jessica, from the rich Jew, a special deed of gift, after his death, of all his worldly goods.
Fair ladies, you drop manna among the starving.

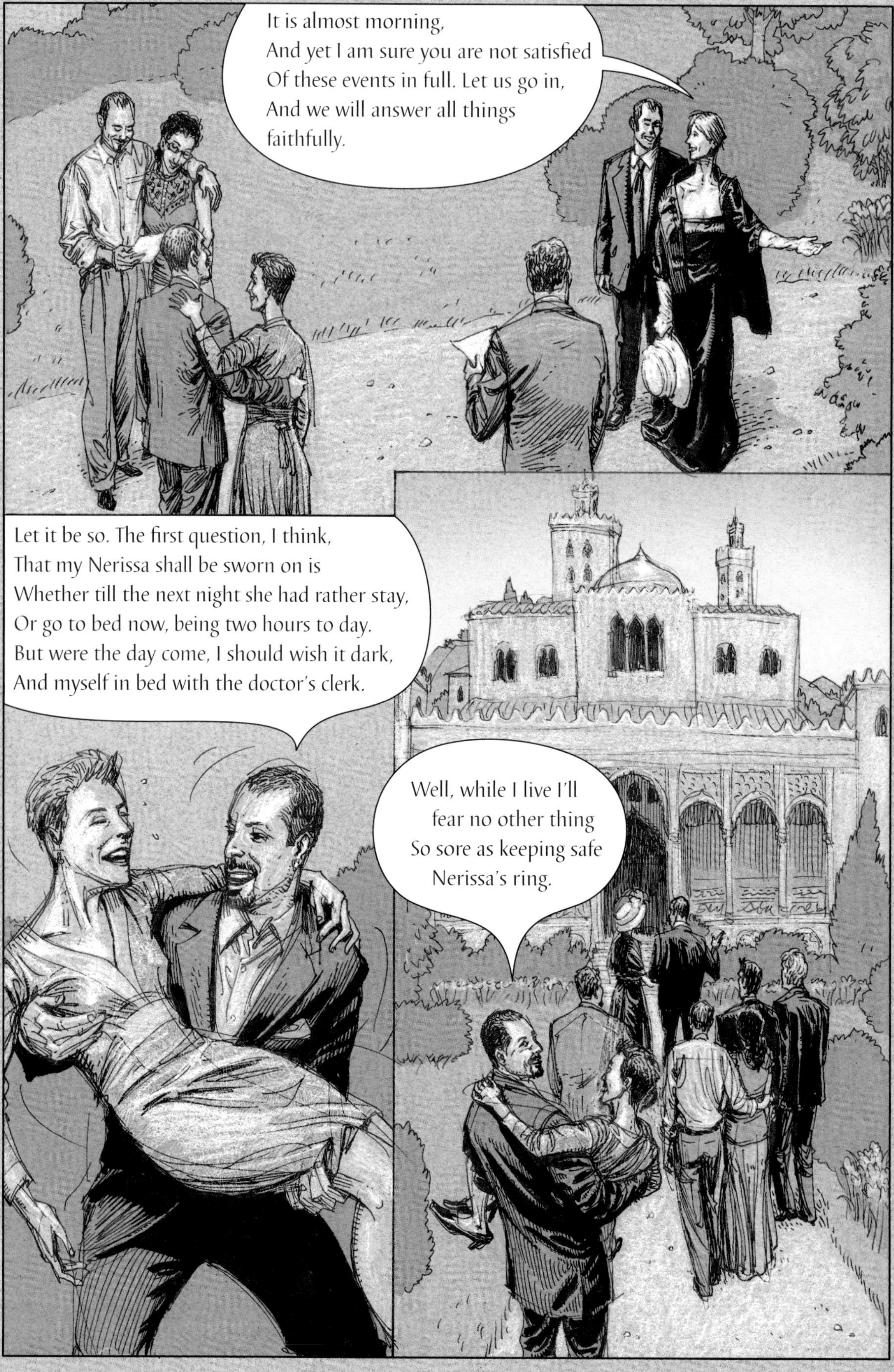
It is almost morning,
And yet I am sure you are not satisfied
Of these events in full. Let us go in,
And we will answer all things
faithfully.
Let it be so. The first question, I think,
That my Nerissa shall be sworn on is
Whether till the next night she had rather stay,
Or go to bed now, being two hours to day.
But were the day come, I should wish it dark,
And myself in bed with the doctor's clerk.
Well, while I live I'll
fear no other thing
So sore as keeping safe
Nerissa's ring.

AUTHOR'S NOTE

The Merchant of Venice is a controversial play. Was Shakespeare racist, or is the play a commentary on racism? Is it anti-Semitic or anti-Christian? What are we to make of the overtones of homosexuality? I am not going to take a position here, but if you are offended or intrigued by any aspect of the story, I encourage you to look further into these questions for yourself. There is a wealth of critical writing on them, and a simple Internet search will give you a good start.

More so than in my previous graphic novels, *Beowulf* and *King Lear*, my *Merchant* text is greatly altered from the original. A large amount of Shakespeare's material has been cut, including whole scenes and characters (such as the high-spirited Launcelot Gobbo and his aged father, depicted below), and many passages have been changed from verse to modern prose. However, when altering the sections that are still in verse, I made a strong effort to preserve the iambic pentameter and the feel of the language.

You may perceive a gradual shift through the course of the book from simpler, more modern prose to unedited Shakespearean verse. This is partly a sneaky way to get readers comfortable with the language, but mainly it is because the most famous speeches in this play occur near the end, in the court scene, and I wanted to preserve those in the original verse as much as possible.

I have chosen to set this book in a modern Venice. Staging Shakespeare in a modern setting is by no means a new idea. Many directors have done it to good effect, but it does inevitably create certain anachronisms, some trivial, some more jarring. In Shakespeare's time both anti-Semitism and slavery were commonplace. To the modern reader they seem alien (I hope). If you find them incongruous when placed in a modern setting, I urge you to consider that today we are still struggling with the same basic issue: man's inhumanity toward his fellow man.

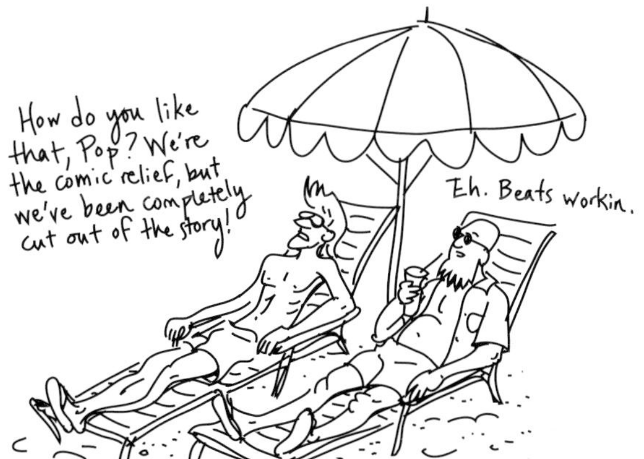
How do you like that, Pop? We're the comic relief, but we've been completely cut out of the story!
Eh. Beats workin.

ACKNOWLEDGMENTS

I drew virtually all the characters in this book from models (posing live when possible, or else photographed). This was something I'd really been wanting to try, and it was a rewarding process despite the huge logistical challenges involved. All the models were my friends, or friends of friends, and I am enormously grateful to all of them for their good-natured hard work—especially the principal "actors," and most particularly "Saint Gayle" for her heroic patience through countless hours of posing as well as the horrors of dress shopping. Models, thank you all. Without you, this would have been a very different book.

Antonio – **Paul Crook**
Bassanio – **Gordon Fontaine**
Gratiano – **Aaron Green**
Salerio – **Salvador Casanas**
Salanio – **Edwin Maas**
Lorenzo – **Juan Diaz**
Shylock (also Tubal) – **Don Davidoff**

Jessica – **Melissa Marver**
Portia – **Gayle DeDe**
Nerissa – **Theodora Van Roijen**
The Prince of Morocco - **Erick Quashie**
The Prince of Aragon – **Kurt Bickenbach**
The Duke of Venice – **Sean Hyde-Moyer**
Portia's servants/musicians – **Sarah Carrier**

Additionally, for their assistance with the casting, I'd like to thank the Van Amsterdam family, Kelly Garvin, Kim Wutkiewicz, Wes Carroll, Mat MacKenzie, and Dianne Cowan. Mat and Diane also helped with early feedback on the script and layout, as did Joanne Greenberg and Paul Crook. Thanks also to Bruce Borham for his hospitality in Venice, Heather Glista for costume consulting, and Dave Merrill for Nerissa's manly hairstyle.

A very special thank-you to Alison Morris for constant support and help with casting, feedback, coloring, and a thousand other things.

I first read *Merchant* in a class at the New School under the outstanding instruction of Professor Arnold Klein. Preserved in the margins of my dog-eared copy of the play are many keen observations on the recurring themes and symbols in the play, and I thought I'd leave you with a small display of them—with all due credit and thanks to Mr. Klein.

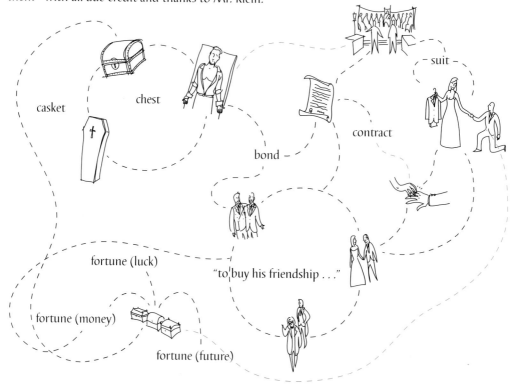

casket

chest

suit

contract

bond –

fortune (luck)

"to buy his friendship . . ."

fortune (money)

fortune (future)

Copyright © 2008 by Gareth Hinds

First paperback edition 2008

Library of Congress Cataloging-in-Publication Data is available.

Library of Congress Catalog Card Number 2007938349

ISBN 978-0-7636-3024-9 (hardcover)
ISBN 978-0-7636-3025-6 (paperback)

2 4 6 8 10 9 7 5 3 1

Printed in Singapore

This book was typeset in Barbedor.

Candlewick Press
2067 Massachusetts Avenue
Cambridge, Massachusetts 02140

visit us at www.candlewick.com

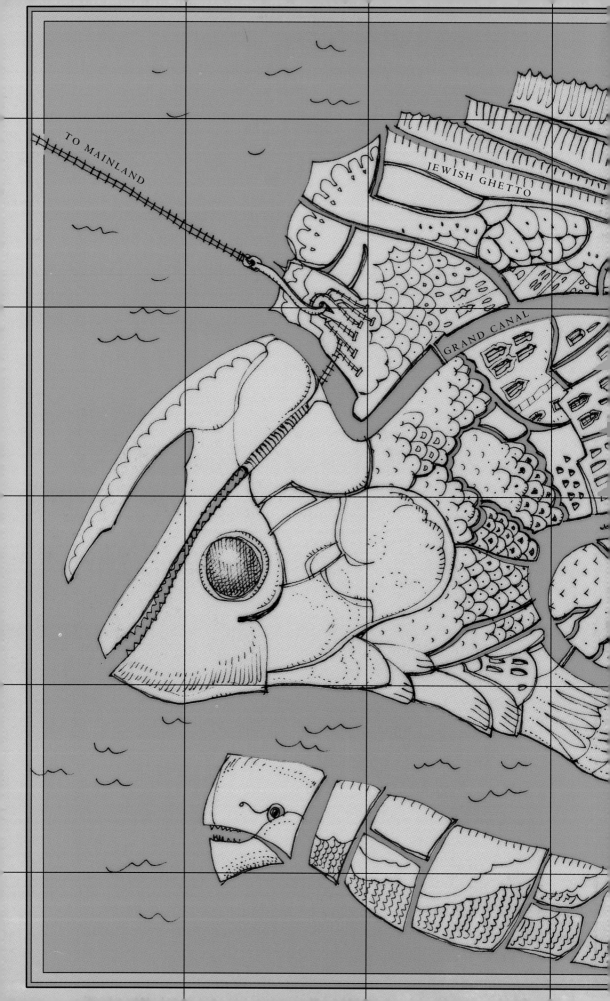

TO MAINLAND

JEWISH GHETTO

GRAND CANAL

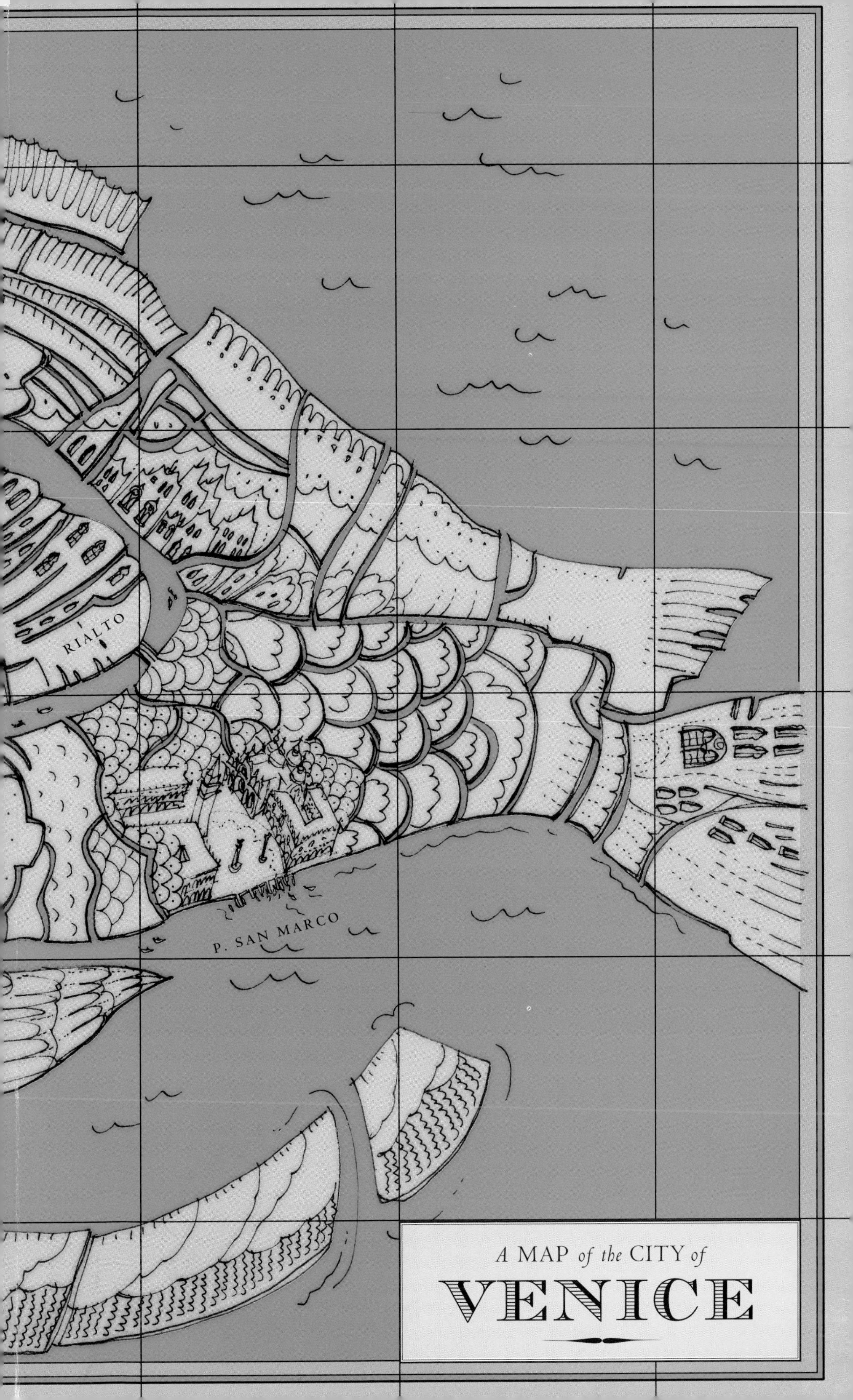
RIALTO
P. SAN MARCO
A MAP of the CITY of
VENICE